NIKKI POWERGLOVES

A Hero is Born

David Estes

This book is dedicated to kids all over the world,
for dreaming BIG,
believing in superheroes,
and loving reading!

Adventures

1	The man-eating porcupine beaver	7
2	The disappearing path into the haunted forest	11
3	Nikki and Mr. Miyagi go on an adventure	14
4	Nikki gets insulted by a Weeble	22
5	Powergloves: Just a cheesy, fashion accessory, or a source of magical power?	28
6	Kids with powers should stick together	35
7	Flying makes you hungry	37
8	Nikki creates a BIG storm	41
9	The dangers of powers	47
10	The gorilla photographer	52
11	I know your secret	58
12	Destroying things is fun	61
13	Spencer gets a shock (of the electrical variety)	63
14	Nikki licks Spencer's face	76
15	Spencer pees his pants, nearly	82
16	Powerbracelets: pretty AND useful	91
17	Nikki becomes a farmer (minus the overalls)	93
18	Ponytails: childish hairdo, or secret identity?	96
19	The t-shirt genius	102
20	Nikki saves Betsy	109
21	Russian spies looking for Nikki?	113
22	The bomb	117
23	Nikki blows up a lake	123
24	From hero to zero	128
25	Getting hit in the head by a lightning bolt hurts	135

26	How to save a villain	141
27	Villains never give up	145
Hero	Hero/Villain Cards	150

1

The man-eating porcupine-beaver

Nikki Nickerson hated her name. Not so much her first name, Nikki was fine, but when combined with Nickerson it was dreadful! What were her mom and dad thinking? The only thing that saved her from constant teasing at school was a boy named George George. His name was definitely worse than hers, but having the second worst name at school was still nothing to be proud of. When she grew up, one of the first things she would do would be to change her name to something cool, like Shakira or Elektra.

Nikki was also bored of being nine-years-old. Nothing exciting ever happened in her life. She hated to complain, because her life wasn't too bad as far as lives go; she lived in a small, but nice house, with a small, but nice family. Without any brothers or sisters, Nikki had to entertain herself much of the time during the long summer holiday from school.

First, she tried playing with friends from school, but all the girls ever wanted to do was try on their moms' makeup and pretend that they were older than they really were. When she asked the boys if she could play with them, they refused; building forts and wrestling was far too difficult for a girl to do, they told her.

Next she tried TV, but her mom said, "That stuff will rot your brain, Nikki. Go outside."

So outside she went, ready to explore the world! After two hours, she realized that there wasn't much to see in her little town of Cragglyville. She visited the old museum, but when she tried to touch one of the Native American exhibits, the security man said, "No touching. Get lost, kid!"

She wanted to get lost. At least getting lost would be more exciting than her life, but instead she decided to go down to the old mill on the river. That proved to be even more boring than the museum; she wasn't allowed inside, and watching the waterwheel churn the muddy water was only cool for about the first five minutes.

She left the mill and went back to town to see if she could get into trouble there.

Like Nikki's house and family, the town of Cragglyville was small, but nice. The roads were kept clean by a weekly street sweeper and the sidewalks were tended to by Old Man Smithy, the local litter collector. The layout of the town was basic; the flat topography allowed a grid pattern to be used, with one main street running down the town center—the name of the road was Main Street, no joke—while various cross streets intersected it at one block intervals. The town had a rustic feel to it, like it had never been touched by the Industrial Revolution. At any second, one might expect a gang of outlaws to ride up on their black horses and start a gunfight with the local sheriff. Surprisingly, there were no tumbleweeds bouncing along Main Street, but mainly because Smithy was so good at his job.

The town had one of each of the basic necessities: a post office for snail-mail; a Town Hall for government functions; a bakery for tasty treats; a diner for coffee, flapjacks, and gossip—the coffee and pancakes were good, but the gossip was the tastiest of all—a police station to keep order; a hospital for bumps, bruises and the flu; and a bank, of course, as an alternative for keeping your money in a piggy-bank or under your mattress.

Nikki had just walked past the old bank, which was on the corner of Main Street and Rooster Road, when she stopped and scratched her head. *Robbing a bank could be exciting*, she thought. She could be like Jessie James and Billy the Kid. An outlaw, always one step ahead of the law! No way, the much wiser part of her brain said, your parents will ground you for a month if you rob a bank.

So robbing a bank was out. That left what? A whole lot of nothing, that's what. Nikki decided to head for home to see if she could find a tree to climb or a bike to ride.

Upon reaching Plantation Road, she cut across the street and off of the sidewalk, opting to take the "short" cut, along the edge of the woods and around the cornfields. In reality, this route wasn't really shorter, but Nikki found it far more interesting than walking on the same roads, past the same houses.

While she walked along, Nikki picked up a sturdy branch that had fallen from a tree overhanging the fields. Using it as a hiking stick, she imagined that she was a famous explorer discovering the land for the first time. "Discovering what?" she asked herself out loud. *A bunch of cornfields*, she thought, *not very exciting at all*. She needed to find an adventure to have!

Nikki stopped and gazed at the endless rows of corn marching into the distance. She hated corn—the look, the taste, the feel. Yuck! Turning in the other direction, toward the woods, she peered into the gloom. How could it be so dark in there when it was so bright outside? The sun rose high above her and she was hot and sweaty from trudging all over town. The forest looked cool and quiet. A light breeze wafted through the crisscross of branches, slowly moving them up and down, as if they were inviting her into their world.

There was a rumor going around school that the forest was haunted. By what, no one knew, but the kids were sure that it was dangerous. *Maybe something dangerous is exactly what I need*, Nikki thought. "No,

Nikki," the responsible part of her mind said. "It is far too dangerous and your parents would not want you to go in there."

"Be quiet, why can't I have any fun?" Nikki muttered to herself. She took another long look at the forest before allowing the cowardly part of her brain to win the argument. Just as she began to walk away, she heard a loud cracking sound from the trees behind her.

She froze.

Slowly turning her head, she looked to see what had caused the noise. That's when she saw the path. It was not some small, overgrown trail that you might expect to see leading into a forest, but instead, was a wide, clear corridor. Nikki had passed by this way a hundred times before and had never seen this path. Where had it come from?

The ground was almost completely free of branches and leaves, like it had been swept clean by a caretaker, or maybe Smithy; it was as smooth as the marble floor in an art gallery. And sitting directly in the center of the path was a large, fat animal, resembling a cross between a porcupine and a beaver. The furry mammal was sitting atop a broken branch, having fallen from the trees high above. So this was the source of the cracking sound, Nikki realized.

The animal growled, its mouth opening wide to reveal several sets of razor sharp teeth.

2

The disappearing path into the
haunted forest

Nikki ran harder than she had ever run. She tripped once, scrambled to her feet, and tripped again. Her legs felt like jelly. Lying face down on the ground, she waited to be torn to shreds by the savage beast. Twenty seconds passed, and then thirty, but the attack never came.

A million questions rattled through Nikki's brain like, "What if the animal is just really slow and is still coming after me?" or, "I wonder what it feels like to be dinner for a man-eating porcupine-beaver?"

Wanting to find out whether she was still being chased, Nikki rolled over onto her back and sat up, pulling her legs under her to sit cross-legged on the ground. She looked back toward the woods where the path had first appeared. Scanning the tree line, she couldn't see the opening anymore. She would need to take a closer look.

Nikki marched bravely back to the forest and crept along the edge, watching for any signs of movement. After she had tiptoed about a hundred steps or so, she realized that the path into the forest had disappeared.

***

Later that day, Nikki lay on her bed staring at the ceiling. Her mind raced back to the cornfields, to the cracking noise, to the mysterious disappearing path, and finally, to the strange animal with the shark-like teeth. Had she imagined it?

A low whine sounded from under her arm. She jumped, startled by the noise. "Oh, Mr. Miyagi, I'm sorry. I forgot you were there." Mr. Miyagi was Nikki's dog. He had been hers since she was five-years-old and so, for the last four years, they had grown up together. The playful and obedient Scottie was named after the famous karate instructor from the movie, *The Karate Kid*. As she gently stroked the fur of her black Scottish terrier, she wondered again whether the events of the day had just been a particularly imaginative daydream.

Nikki's mom regularly told her that she had an especially overactive imagination, and that sometimes she needed to focus more on what was real. Nikki wished that her best friend, Spencer, was with her, because he could've been a second witness to the unbelievable story.

Nikki had known Spencer Quick her entire life. He lived on the same street, went to the same school, and liked doing the same things as she did. Sadly, his parents had divorced three years earlier and so, each summer he spent a month with his dad, who lived in New York. He had only been gone for a week so far, but Nikki already missed him very much. She needed to tell him what had happened.

Grabbing her cell phone from the bedside table, she found Spencer's name in her address book and pressed the CALL button. The satisfying chirp of the phone ringing clucked in her ear. After three rings with no answer, Nikki began muttering, "Pick up, pick up, pick up. C'mon, Spencer!"

On the fourth ring, she heard the call connect and a voice say, "ET phone home! Hi, Nikks."

Frustrated, Nikki said, "What took you so long to answer, Spence?"

"Oh, sorry about that. I was just watching ET on TV with my dad. I can't stay on for too long, we're having an intermission so he can scoop some ice cream for us while I talk to you."

Nikki's stomach growled. Ice cream sounded good. She had barely touched her food at dinner, because she was too worried about what had happened, but now her appetite came roaring back at Spencer's mention of her favorite cold treat. "That's okay, Spence. But listen, I have an emergency here that I need your advice for."

"Okay, shoot."

Nikki rushed through the story and waited for his reply. She heard him humming to himself. Spencer always hummed whenever he was thinking hard about something; he said it was his way of concentrating. In the background, she heard a voice yell, "Spencerrrr! Come on back down now, your ice cream's melting!"

"Oh shoot, I gotta go, woowoo!" he said. "Listen, don't do anything until I get back to Cragglyville. We can figure things out together."

"Spence, that's three weeks away, I don't think I can wait that long!" Nikki practically shrieked.

"Just try, okay? Gotta run. Over and out." Before she could respond, he had hung up and she could hear the monotonous drone of the dial tone in her ear.

"Well that just stinks," Nikki complained to herself. She slumped down on her bed and flipped over onto her stomach to think things through. Surely there couldn't be a dangerous animal roaming freely in their little forest. Nikki had never heard of any animal attacks in Cragglyville. "I don't care if Spencer wants me to wait for him," Nikki mumbled, as a plan began to form in her head.

3

Nikki and Mr. Miyagi go on an adventure

The next day, Nikki jumped out of bed at seven o'clock in the morning, threw on some clothes, brushed her teeth, made her bed, and bounded down the stairs with Mr. Miyagi hot on her heels. She hadn't felt so excited for the start of a new day since summer began two weeks earlier.

"Aren't you an early bird today," Nikki's mom said when she saw her daughter practically burst into the kitchen.

"Uh, yeah, Mom. I'm just taking your advice and getting outside to enjoy the summer," Nikki answered tentatively—her mom could usually see straight through her lies.

This time she didn't though.

"That's great, Nikki. If you come back around noon, I can make you lunch when I get back from my book club."

Mrs. Nickerson was short, with shoulder-length, reddish-brown hair. An eternal optimist, she was always able to find the silver lining in even the worst situations. She was a stay-at-home mom who, once Nikki started school, began to join clubs to keep herself busy. Not just a couple of clubs, but a club for every day of the week. She had running club on Mondays, Spanish club on Wednesdays, arts and crafts club on Thursdays, dog training club on Fridays, and bridge club on Saturdays, where she played a weird card game that Nikki didn't understand at all. She even joined a chess club that met on Sundays. Today was Tuesday, which was book club day.

Nikki thought that her mom overdid it a bit, but her activities seemed to make her happy, so Nikki didn't say anything. Her mom constantly invited Nikki to come along, but as a rule, she always said no. What nine-year-old girl wanted to hang out with a bunch of old people doing boring things? There was only one exception to her rule: dog training club.

Nikki went with her mom to dog training club as often as possible. She loved watching all of the different breeds learn skills, from as basic as sitting or rolling over, to as complex as collecting the newspaper or pushing a stroller. There was even a particularly clever collie that had learned how to press the speed dial for emergency services on her owner's cell phone. Mr. Miyagi was somewhere in the middle of his training class and Nikki hoped that one day he would be the smartest dog in the club.

"Sounds great, Mom, but I may just take my allowance for the week and buy something in town." Nikki tried to avoid eye contact as she poured her cereal, added extra sugar, and filled a bowl with minced beef kibbles for Mr. Miyagi.

"Okay, sweetie, but be careful and don't be home too late."

"Sure," Nikki said, stuffing a large spoonful of Cheerios into her mouth. She crunched loudly, appreciative of the first few bites of cereal, before the milk made the small O's too mushy to crunch. Her mom turned back to the local newspaper she was reading.

"Hmmm," Mrs. Nickerson murmured, reacting to something she had read.

"What is it, Mom?" Nikki asked in between mouthfuls.

"Nothing really, it's just the usual problems with the groundhogs getting into Farmer Miller's cornfields again. But the odd thing is that the bite marks on the damaged ears they found are different than what a groundhog's teeth usually look like. Apparently they are much sharper looking. Isn't that strange?"

Nikki's mouth stopped chewing in mid-bite. *Sharp bite marks! Farmer Miller's cornfield! That's where she had seen the creature!* Trying to keep a straight face, Nikki replied, "Yeah, that's strange, Mom. Do they think it could be a different kind of animal?"

Her mom shrugged. "They're not sure yet, but it's probably nothing to worry about. If the animal is eating corn, then it's probably just an herbivore anyway."

Nikki's heart skipped a beat. Why hadn't she thought of that? If it was eating corn it must be a veggie-eater. That would also explain why the pudgy creature hadn't chased her. It had probably just growled because it was afraid of her. Having no reason to be scared now, she became even more eager to investigate the hidden path into the forest.

Skipping the last few bites of cereal, she emptied her bowl down the garbage disposal and rushed for the door.

"Wait just one minute, young lady, aren't you forgetting something?" her mom asked.

Nikki tried to remember each of her chores and whether she had done them. Make her bed, check. Brush her teeth, check. Clean her room, check. Her mind drew a blank.

Her mom gave her a clue: "Well, besides saying goodbye to me, isn't there a certain four-legged furry creature that needs some attention?"

Nikki's jaw dropped, thinking that her mom was referring to the animal from the forest. Then she remembered. Mr. Miyagi. "Oops! Sorry, Mom, I forgot to walk him. Maybe I could just take him with me for the day?"

Mrs. Nickerson thought about it for a minute and then said, "You know what, Nikks, I think that's a great idea, just make sure you keep him on the leash and that he gets plenty of water. Here, I'll pack you a bag of doggie treats in case he gets hungry."

Nikki added the dog supplies to her small backpack, kissed her mom goodbye, and held the door to let Mr. Miyagi out. He scampered through the doorway and down the stairs, and then waited obediently for her to catch up when he reached the end of his leash.

The pair jogged down the street and past Spencer's house. His voice from the night before rang in her ear: *Don't do anything until I get back…we can figure things out together.* She tried to ignore the voice in her head and continued to the end of the block and around the corner. Once out of her neighborhood, she turned left on Plantation Road, but instead of going all the way to the end, she led Mr. Miyagi off the road to the right before they reached Farmer Miller's place.

Crazy Miller, as the kids at school called him, was a stern, giant of a man, who had earned his reputation for being a bit loony by chasing children out of his garden with a pitchfork. Even though he appeared to be childless, there was a rumor going around that he kept four or five kids locked up in his barn to use as manual labor for his farm. A common dare amongst the boys in her grade was to see who could get the closest to touching his barn before freaking out and running away.

Nikki, on the other hand, knew Mr. Miller well, as he had been a friend of the family for as long as she could remember. Contrary to the talk at school, he was a nice man, and he and his wife would regularly stop by the Nickerson's house to deliver freshly made apple and pumpkin pies. Nikki was one of the few children that Mr. Miller would allow to walk around his fields, and she took great pride in having the privilege to do so.

Just as Nikki and her dog started past the first few rows of corn, Nikki heard a loud voice boom, "Helloooooo, Nikkiiiii!" A smile burst onto her face as she whipped her head around in the direction of the sound.

Farmer Miller was pushing a wheelbarrow filled with sacks of something along the edge of the cornfield. As he approached, Mr.

Miyagi strained at the leash. "Be patient, little one," Nikki cooed. "Your friend will be here in a second." Every time Mr. Miyagi saw Farmer Miller he reacted the same way—it could only be described as sheer excitement. It made sense because every time Farmer Miller was near Nikki's dog, he shamefully spoiled him with belly rubs and doggie treats.

"Hi, Mr. Miller," Nikki said when he arrived.

"Hi there, Nikks. What are you up to on this beautiful, sunny day? Not getting into any trouble are you?" As he spoke, Mr. Miller lowered the heavy-looking wheelbarrow to the ground. His powerful arm muscles were bulging from the effort and he was sweating so much that the salty liquid had soaked straight through his bright red t-shirt and dusty overalls.

While Nikki wasn't scared of Farmer Miller like the other kids were, she couldn't help but treat him with the utmost respect, considering he was about four times the size of her. Looking up at him now, she felt tiny, like an ant that could be squashed with a single step. Her head barely reached his waist, and each of his legs was as thick as her entire body. But when she looked at his face, she saw a kind, caring man. A gentle giant. His eyes twinkled and his smile was cheerful and happy.

"No, Mr. Miller. We were just going on an adventure."

"Ahh, I see." Although it seemed impossible, his eyes twinkled even more and his smile widened even broader. "An adventure, huh? I used to go on quite a few of those myself. Many years ago…." He gazed wistfully into the distant fields, as if a flood of memories had just rushed into his head.

Nikki waited patiently for him to continue. And waited. And waited. Finally, when it appeared he might just stare into the fields all day, Nikki said, "Uh, Mr. Miller?"

His head jerked toward her, like she had surprised him out of a deep, deep sleep. "Sorry, Nikks. I was just thinking about something."

"That's okay. But we better get going as we have a lot to do today."

"Hold on now. You can't possibly walk through my fields without joining me for a piece of apple pie and some fresh squeezed apple cider."

"It's not even eight in the morning yet, Mr. Miller."

"We're not talking about whiskey here. It's never too early for some pie and cider, Nikks. Just don't tell your mom, okay?" He winked at her, his smile returning wider than ever.

Nikki grinned. "I won't."

With a big scoop of his arm, he picked Mr. Miyagi up and placed him on top of the sacks in the wheelbarrow. The dog wagged his tail happily.

As they walked toward the farmhouse, Nikki asked, "What's in these sacks anyway?"

"Seeds. For the veggie garden. Time to start plantin' again," he replied.

"Oh."

Upon arriving at the house, the door opened and a plump, smiling woman emerged. Her hands were covered by oven mitts and she wore a neat, simple red apron. "Hi, Nikki!" she said enthusiastically.

"Hi, Mrs. Miller," Nikki replied. "I couldn't slip by without Mr. Miller inviting me over."

"Well, he's right, of course. Without your help, we would never be able to eat all these pies I've been baking. And then I would grow as big as the house!"

Nikki laughed. The Millers were always able to make her laugh. She had never heard either of them say anything mean to each other or to her, or anyone else for that matter. They were good people. The kind of people you wanted to spend time with.

Twenty minutes and two pieces of apple pie, a glass of cider, and a whole lot of laughs later, Nikki had forgotten all about adventures and strange, toothy creatures, until Farmer Miller said, "I'd better get out there and start plantin'. I have a full day ahead of me. And I still have to set traps for those darn groundhogs."

Nikki's eyes widened. *Groundhogs!* "What groundhogs, Mr. Miller?" she asked, pretending that she hadn't heard the news.

"Oh, it's nothing to worry about, honey. They've only eaten a few ears of corn so far, but if I don't stop them they'll devour every last kernel."

"Oh." She grabbed her backpack and Mr. Miyagi's leash and said, "Thanks again for the pie, it was really yummy. See you later!"

"Bye, dear," Mrs. Miller said. "Don't be a stranger."

"And don't get into any trouble," Mr. Miller added.

"I won't," Nikki promised, replying to both of them.

She dashed out the door, with Mr. Miyagi's little legs scrambling to keep up. Now that her mind was back on her plans, her heart began to beat faster, in anticipation of the adventure that was possibly just around the corner. In her head, she reminded herself that there was nothing to be scared of, because the animal she had seen was probably just as docile as her very own pet. As she approached the forest, she tried to act normal, like she was just passing through, with the hope that the events of the previous day would repeat themselves.

Knowing that they had to be close to the exact spot she had stopped the last time, Nikki stopped again, and tiptoed toward the edge of the forest. Without warning, her typically quiet and even-tempered dog began barking madly, while pulling the leash, along with Nikki, back away from the trees.

"Mr. Miyagi! What's gotten in to you?" Nikki shouted. "Quiet, quiet! I'm moving back now!"

As soon as she stepped away from the border between the field and the trees, Mr. Miyagi stopped barking, sat down on his hind legs, and acted completely normal, as if he had just been sitting patiently the entire time. Nikki crouched next to him and stroked him under the chin, "What's the matter, puppy?" she asked.

Her bearded friend just looked at her, his tongue hanging out of his mouth in response to the hot, sunny day. "Are you thirsty?" Nikki guessed. She unzipped her backpack and pulled out a bottle of water and a small dish she had brought.

Mr. Miyagi greedily emptied the bowl nearly as fast as his owner filled it, while Nikki gulped down the rest of the bottle. Without warning, a sharp cracking sound rose from the forest. Nikki whipped her head around to see what had caused it. Sure enough, a wide trail had magically appeared, with the peculiar, roundish animal balanced on a broken branch in the middle of the entrance.

Mr. Miyagi leapt from his haunches and charged for the path, ripping the leash from Nikki's loose grip. Time began to move in slow motion as Nikki clambered to her feet and raced after him, yelling, "Nooo, Mr. Miyagi! Come back!!" Her usually responsive dog ignored her request and raced straight for the creature, which seemed completely unperturbed by the streaking canine headed its way.

Just before the Scottie collided with it, the animal deftly rolled to the side, out of harm's way. Mr. Miyagi skidded to a stop, and before he could turn to charge again, the creature rolled off down the path, much faster than Nikki would have thought possible from such a pudgy little mammal. Within seconds it was out of sight; the only evidence that it had ever been there at all was the broken branch and a tiny track in the dirt, left by its pointy fur as it rolled down the trail, like a bowling ball headed for a cluster of pins.

Mr. Miyagi stood still and stared into the forest, his tail wagging expectantly, as if he believed the animal would return as quickly as it had left. Finally catching up, Nikki slowly picked up the leash, regaining control of her pet. She glanced at her blue waterproof watch and saw that it was not even nine o'clock in the morning yet! She hadn't been awake for two hours and already her day had more excitement than she had ever had in her entire life. *This is shaping up to be the best day ever*, she thought.

Nikki sat down to think about what to do next. One thing was certain: She would follow the animal's tracks, even if it took her directly into the face of danger.

4

Nikki gets insulted by a Weeble

Nikki waited only five minutes before making a decision. She would follow the creature's trail, and she would bring her dog with her for protection and companionship.

First, she tied the end of his leash around her wrist, so that he couldn't yank it free again—the last thing she needed was for her dog to get lost in the dark forest. Next, she opened her bag and pulled out two doggie biscuits, which Mr. Miyagi scarfed down, despite the fact that he had just eaten breakfast. She opened a second water bottle and quenched her thirst; her throat had become quite dry from chasing Mr. Miyagi.

After zipping her bag shut, she picked up the branch that had fallen from the tree and inspected it. It was strong and would do quite well for a walking stick, and could probably be used as a weapon if she encountered anything dangerous. There were a couple of balls of fur stuck to the wood, proof that the branch had recently been used as a perch by the fat, furry animal.

Ready to go, Nikki said, "C'mon, boy, let's go!" and led Mr. Miyagi down the arrow-straight trail, which aimed directly into the forest. As they walked, she took in her surroundings, trying to remember anything that might be important. She was a real explorer now and she had a responsibility to document anything that she discovered during her adventure.

For the first mile or so, she didn't see anything out of the ordinary, just trees and bushes and an occasional butterfly, which Mr. Miyagi desperately tried to chase, but Nikki held his tether tight and he was forced to continue along with her.

Eventually, the path descended downwards, twisting and turning around tree stumps and roots. It also narrowed, until there was barely enough room for her and her dog to walk side by side. Nikki's mind was focused on the strange creature. It looked like a porcupine because of its spiky fur, but had the face and tail of a beaver. The name porcupine-beaver was too long for such a small animal. "Hmm..." Nikki mused. "I think I will call you Beaverpine," she said out loud.

Nikki kept her eyes on the path now, as it was more difficult to see the tracks of the rolling Beaverpine. Abruptly, the trail ended into a small, circular clearing. Directly in the center was the Beaverpine, and as soon as Mr. Miyagi saw it, he strained at the leash, trying to break free. Nikki pulled the leash tight and gradually reeled her dog in, until he was within reach. She scooped him up and whispered in his ear, "It's okay, Mr. Miyagi. Don't worry, we're just going to go and try to make friends with it."

Obediently, her dog stopped squirming and allowed Nikki to hold him. She peered at the Beaverpine, which stared straight back at her, motionless and unblinking. Although Nikki wanted to approach the Beaverpine, she paused when she noticed that it appeared to be sitting on something. Nikki could tell that it was some kind of a container, wooden maybe, and that it was much larger than a shoebox. The first thing that popped into her head was: *a treasure chest!*

Nikki's first reaction was to run over, knock the Beaverpine off and open the chest to see what was inside. But she knew that was not a very smart idea and so, instead, she slowly walked toward the animal, which seemed to be guarding the chest. As she approached, Nikki talked in a gentle baby voice to the creature, like she always talked to Mr. Miyagi.

"Don't worry, little one, we're not going to hurt you. We just want to make friends and see what you are hiding."

When she got within ten feet, the previously silent animal commanded, "Be quiet already! I'm not some child or pet; speak to me like a normal person!"

Stunned, Nikki stopped dead in her tracks. *Did the Beaverpine just talk to her?* While Nikki had always believed that she was able to communicate with Mr. Miyagi on some level, she had never heard of any animals that could actually speak like humans do, except for a parrot, of course, which could only imitate human speech.

Not knowing what to say, Nikki just stared at it.

"Do you or do you not want to find out why I have brought you here?" the Beaverpine asked. Its voice was gruff, and Nikki thought she could detect a slight New York accent.

Nikki found her voice and stammered, "Yes, uh, yes, sir. I would very much like to know why I am here, but I think you are a bit confused. You see, you didn't bring us here, we followed you."

The Beaverpine rolled his eyes and chuckled, "Followed me! Ha! You couldn't follow Tyrannosaurus Rex through a meadow of freshly fallen snow! I left you obvious tracks to allow you to find this place. I *led* you here."

Nikki was getting a bit annoyed with the insults from a beast that could barely reach her knees. "Okay, Mister Smarty Pants, how did you know I was going to follow you at all?"

"Ahhh, now you are asking good questions, my dear. I was beginning to fear I had chosen the wrong girl. I knew you would follow me, because you have been chosen to receive a very special gift, as you are brave and adventurous and have a good heart."

Nikki's eyes lit up upon hearing his compliments. "You're right, Mr. Beaverpine, I am all of those things! When you say gift, do you mean the treasure you are guarding?"

"First of all, I am a Weeble, not a Beaverpine, but yes, of course, Nikki. This chest is yours to open, if you choose to. But a word of advice: You cannot open the chest if you are not willing to accept the sacrifices that come with the great responsibility attached to the treasures inside."

Nikki wondered why she had never heard of an animal called a Weeble, but chose to ignore it for now. "Thank you for your concern, sir, but if I am everything you say I am, I should be able to handle whatever is inside."

"As you wish," the Weeble said, rolling off of the box. In a flash, the Weeble had rolled out of the clearing and disappeared into the dense forest.

"That was weird," Nikki said to Mr. Miyagi, who had watched the conversation in silence. When she set him down, he tore over to the chest and began sniffing around its base.

Nikki followed her pet and inspected the container closely. The chest was beautiful. It was a bright gold color with silver trim and appeared to be metal, until Nikki touched it and found it to be quite soft and spongy. It was also warm on all sides, like an old pair of jeans that had just come out of the dryer. There were intricate carvings on each side, as well as the lid. They looked ancient, like something you would see in a museum. The pictures showed children doing amazing things. One was flying through the air without wings or a cape or anything. Another was lifting a huge stone block above her head. There was even one that seemed to be shooting lightning out of his fingertips.

"I have to get this open," Nikki said to Mr. Miyagi.

First she tried lifting the lid straight off, but it wouldn't budge. Next, she tried poking her walking stick underneath the lid to pry it off, but all she did was crack the tip of the branch. Not wanting to damage the chest, but having no other choice, she found a large rock and smashed it into the lid, hoping she could break it to get inside. But the rock crumbled as soon as it touched the lid, like it was a piece of chalk, rather than a hard stone.

In frustration, Nikki kicked the chest and then grabbed her foot when pain shot through her toes. "Owww! Why won't this stupid thing open?!" she yelled.

Not knowing what else to do, Nikki sat on the lid, exactly where the Weeble had been sitting. She needed to think. Mr. Miyagi pawed in the dirt at the side of the box; he seemed to be trying to dig his way under and through the bottom. Nikki considered telling him to stop, but she knew he was just trying to help so she let him continue.

Why would that darn Weeble leave her with a chest that he said she had been chosen to receive, and not tell her how to open it? Perhaps she had been too quick to dismiss his advice about being willing to accept the responsibility of the treasure. That's when it dawned on her. A magical treasure chest surely could not be opened by conventional means. The Weeble had said that she wouldn't be able to open it unless she was willing to accept the sacrifices that came along with the treasure. She was willing, but maybe she needed to make that very clear.

When she stepped off of the box, Mr. Miyagi stopped digging and looked at her curiously. She took one big step back and with her dog at her feet, proceeded to say in a loud voice, "Oh, magical treasure chest, I am willing to accept the sacrifices and the responsibility that come along with whatever gifts you hold inside of you!"

To her utter amazement, the chest lifted off the ground and began to glow bright gold, sparks flying from the lid. It began to spin, slowly at first, and then faster and faster, until Nikki became dizzy from watching it. When it seemed that it couldn't possibly go any faster, the lid popped off with a sharp crack, similar to the sound she had heard when the disappearing pathway into the forest had first appeared.

Once opened, the chest crashed to the ground, gravity once more gaining its hold. Nikki approached the glowing container and peered over the edge.

5

Powergloves: Just a cheesy, fashion accessory, or a source of magical power?

Disappointment, anger, frustration. Those were just a few of the emotions that Nikki felt when she saw what the treasure chest contained. In her mind she was expecting gold, silver, maybe even diamonds, but instead all she got was a pile of gloves. Of all things, gloves! There were about a dozen different varieties in various colors, each with a drawing on them, similar to the ones on the outside of the box.

Nikki picked up one pair. They were white with gold trim and felt rubbery to the touch. Printed on the glove was a single snowflake. *How boring*, Nikki thought. They almost looked like the type of gloves her mother used to clean with to prevent chemicals from touching her skin.

The gloves were hers now so she figured that she should at least try them on to see if they even fit. They looked way too big for her, like they were meant for an adult. She slipped the first white glove onto her left hand and to her amazement, it fit perfectly! She held the other white glove next to her right hand and could tell that it was much bigger. *Whoever made these gloves really screwed up*, she thought, *they aren't even the same size!*

Just to see what it would look like to wear two different-sized gloves, Nikki slipped her right hand into the second glove. Her eyes widened when the glove hugged her hand and wrist as if it had been custom-made to fit her hand exactly. The glove had magically shrunk without her even noticing. She pressed her thumb onto the drawing of the snowflake and could feel that the picture was created with raised bumps, like the braille books that the blind boy at her school had shown her.

Curious to see if the other gloves would fit her too, Nikki reached into the chest to find another pair. As she leaned over the large box, Mr. Miyagi ran underneath her feet and startled her, causing her to fall to the ground. Nikki reached one hand down to catch her fall, and as she did, there was a sudden flash of white and then she was sliding across the ground out of control. She finally stopped when she crashed into a bush on the edge of the clearing.

Nikki looked for Mr. Miyagi and found that he had also slid across the clearing, but to the other side. "What was that?" she wondered aloud. And why were her legs so cold? Mr. Miyagi barked once and tried to run toward her, his little legs sliding backwards with each step. Eventually he was able to get enough traction to move forward, but after three steps he had lost control completely, so he sat down and allowed his forward motion to propel him to where Nikki was sitting.

"Mr. Miyagi, look out!" Nikki yelled, already knowing it was too late for him to change his trajectory. Nikki let out an "Oommff!" as she caught her dog just as he smashed into her stomach. He licked her face happily, oblivious to the strange events that had just transpired.

Nikki sat up and looked around the clearing. The ground had a glossy shimmer to it and shined brightly, reflecting the sun's rays. She touched the ground. It was cold and hard, like ice. *Wait a minute*, she thought, *it is ice!* But how was that possible? It was a warm summer day outside and yet, here she was, sitting on the icy ground, like it was the middle of winter and a pond had frozen over.

It hit her. *The gloves!* She looked at the white gloves with the snowflake prints. When she fell, the gloves must have somehow caused the ice to appear. Questions poured through her mind: Were they magic gloves? Did she cause the ice to appear or did the gloves do it themselves? What about the other gloves, could they do special things, too?

Excited now, Nikki stood up slowly, being careful not to slip, and shuffled her way over to the chest. After pulling the snowflake gloves off, she lay them gently back in the box and pulled out another pair— these ones were bright red and had flames printed on them. *If a snowflake means ice, surely a flame means fire*, she thought.

She put on each of the fire gloves and not surprisingly, they fit exactly to the size of her hands. Not knowing how they worked, Nikki tried pointing them at the ground and yelling, "Fire power!" "Abracadabra!" and "Burn, baby, burn!" but with each command nothing happened.

She even tried pretending to fall to the ground in hopes that they would react like the ice gloves had. But all she gained was a bruised rear end after slamming onto the ice. Perplexed, she stopped to think. What had she done differently the first time? She had taken the white gloves out, looked at them, put them on, and then fallen. Something was missing. Like a light bulb turning on in her head, she realized that she *had* done something else with the white gloves. She had touched the snowflake picture.

Nikki turned her hand palm-side up and just like before, she pressed her thumb to the picture printed on the glove—in this case, the flames. Angling her arm toward the ground, she extended her fingers. Rather than commanding the glove as she had before, she simply thought about fire spewing from the glove. Instantly, her hand was engulfed in fire, and bright red and yellow flames shot from the glove, licking the icy ground below.

In seconds, the ice began to melt into a puddle and a circle of burnt grass appeared. Unsure of how to turn off the gloves, Nikki closed her eyes and tried to picture the glove without the flames coming out of it. When she opened her eyes, the fire had stopped and there was a single wisp of smoke rising from the tip of her pointer finger. *Awesome!* she thought. Spence was never going to believe this! Mr. Miyagi trotted happily over to the small circle of brown grass and lay down. He seemed glad to be off of the cold, slippery ice.

Anxious to see what other powers the remaining gloves would give her, Nikki slipped the red ones off and returned them to the chest, while scooping up the next pair and shoving her hands into them. Again, they were a perfect fit.

These gloves were light blue with a picture of a bird on them. She jammed her thumb onto the bird symbol, closed her eyes, and thought about what it would be like to be a bird. In her mind, she flew high above the trees, the fields, and the houses. She didn't feel anything change and when she opened her eyes, she fully expected to be standing in the same spot, her feet planted firmly on the ground.

To her shock, her body had lifted completely off the ground and was rising through the air, already nearly above the trees. Mr. Miyagi was barking at her from below, but his bark was becoming softer and softer as she rose higher and higher.

Nikki gasped for breath, afraid that she might go up and up forever, until she reached outer space, where she would float off to the moon, the Milky Way, or even further. She closed her eyes and tried to think of herself back on the ground and as soon as she did, her stomach dropped rapidly, like she was on a rollercoaster, her body hurtling down toward the earth below.

She shrieked and began flapping her arms in the hopes that, like a bird, she would be able to propel herself upwards again. But it didn't work and the ground came nearer and nearer. Frantically, Nikki remembered how she had flown in the first place and began to picture herself rising up again.

Her body jerked to a stop and her head snapped forwards, like she was in a car and the driver had just slammed on the brakes. Like before, her body began to rise. Gaining confidence, Nikki extended her arms like she had seen Superman do in the movies, and imagined herself flying through the air. Right on cue, her body stopped rising and shot forward rapidly, her legs thrown behind her.

It didn't take long for Nikki to get the hang of flying; it was as easy as thinking about the next turn or dip or dive that she wanted to make, and her body would react instantly. Time was meaningless as she learned how to do loops, to stop and turn on a ninety-degree angle, and even how to hover in place like a hummingbird.

Flying was every child's dream and Nikki loved every minute of it. She hoped it would never end. She loved the feel of the wind through her hair, the anticipation of the next loop she would perform and the thrill of diving toward the earth at amazing speeds.

Nikki careened over the forest with reckless abandon. At one point she flew close to the edge of the forest and momentarily crossed over one of the surrounding farms. *Oops*, she thought. She had to be careful not to be seen. As she corrected her flight path and turned back toward the forest, she noticed a flash of light from the corner of her eye. She twisted her head in the direction of the flash, and saw a farmer aiming a camera at her. Flash! Another burst of light. Zooming back to the safety of the forest, she tried to calm herself down.

It was okay. Just a photograph. And it was taken from far away, so surely no one would be able to tell who she was. If the farmer tried to tell a story about seeing a flying girl, people would probably think he was crazy. They would take one look at his photo and say it was a bird of some kind. She was safe.

As she reasoned to herself, Nikki noticed that the sun had moved well past its peak. She looked at her watch and was dismayed when she realized how long she had been flying. It was almost five o'clock in the afternoon; she had been in the air for hours!

She needed to get back to the clearing as soon as possible to pick up Mr. Miyagi and walk home. Her mom usually had dinner ready by six o'clock and she would be mad if Nikki was late.

Nikki flew over the forest, in search of the lone clearing amongst the tall trees. Minutes later, she spotted the circle of empty space. Skillfully, she guided her body over the clearing using only her mind, and lowered herself straight down, like a helicopter.

Baking all day in the hot sun, the ice had melted and the ground was soggy. To her relief, Mr. Miyagi was still curled up on the patch of grass that Nikki had burned earlier that day. She bent down and gently stroked his hair and he groggily opened his eyes and licked her face.

"Hee hee, Mr. Miyagi, that tickles," Nikki said, giggling. "It's time to go home, buddy." Her dog scrambled to his feet and followed Nikki back down the path they had taken earlier that day. It seemed like years since they had started their adventure.

A few feet down the trail, Nikki glanced at the light blue gloves she was still wearing and remembered that she was forgetting something. "Oh no, I forgot about the chest!" she exclaimed. "We have to go back."

They returned to where the chest stood wide open, ready for its owner to claim it. "Hmm," Nikki murmured. "How are we going to get this home?" she asked her dog. He just looked at her with his tongue hanging out. *Having Spencer here would be helpful*, Nikki thought.

She tried to lift the chest, but it was very heavy and she couldn't even raise it an inch. "Well, I guess I'll just have to take the gloves and leave the chest," she said, reaching in the box to grab a handful of the multi-colored gloves. When she attempted to pull her hand back out though, it was as if her fingers were stuck in cement; they just wouldn't budge. Nikki tried lifting her arm at different angles and with different amounts of force, but no matter what she tried, her hand was as stuck as a pin cushion.

She released the other gloves and let them drop back into the container and magically, she was able to pull her hand back out. It seemed that only one pair of gloves could be taken from the chest at a time. *I might have to leave them here and return whenever I want to use them*, she thought.

Now, where was the lid? She remembered that it had popped off when the chest first opened, but she never looked to see where it had landed. Nikki walked around the clearing two times, but there was no sign of the lid. Just when she was about to give up, Nikki noticed a gleam of gold out of the corner of her eye. A corner of the lid was peeking out from behind a large tree.

Unable to easily lift it, Nikki half-carried, half-dragged the lid back over to the chest and was barely able to hoist it high enough to slide it back into place. It snapped shut, triggering one more tiny bit of magic. Once closed, the chest bubbled on all sides, like there were creatures trying to push their way through its frame. After five seconds of the strange bubbling, the chest began to shrink right before Nikki's eyes, until it was about the size of the kind of dice that you would use to play Monopoly.

Nikki picked up the tiny chest. "I wonder how I will make you big again. Oh well, I'm sure I will find a way when the time comes." She stuck it into her pocket and then removed the powder blue gloves she was still wearing and shoved them in her backpack for safe keeping. Grabbing Mr. Miyagi's leash, she ran off down the path, hoping she would still make it home in time for dinner.

6

Kids with powers should stick together

Jimmy was hungry. He was hungry a lot. There never seemed to be enough food in the house. But he didn't mind being hungry. He did mind being alone. He had no brothers or sisters. He had a mom, but not a dad. He thought it was weird not to have a dad, but had given up on asking his mom about it because he always got the same answer: "I don't know what to tell you, Jimmy. You just don't have a dad," his mom would always say.

Jimmy was looking out his window at a boy on the street.

Whizzzz! Shoop!

Jimmy's eyes followed the ball.

Whizzzz! Shoop!

The boy looked happy. Really happy. His dad threw the ball back to him.

Whizzzz!

The boy caught it in the pouch of his leather mitt.

Shoop!

Jimmy didn't have a baseball glove. He didn't have a dad either. Sometimes he wished he did. Someone he could talk to, confide in. He couldn't talk to his mom, not really. If he could, he would've told her his secret.

Turning away from the window, Jimmy used one hand to press a button on the remote control and the TV flicked on. Some stupid soap opera. He pressed another button. Just the six o'clock news, boring. He changed the channel one more time. Another news program. But this one was different. Jimmy watched it from time to time because it had a segment called "UFOs around the globe." The show was all about possible alien sightings in the form of Unidentified Flying Objects, or UFOs for short. The UFO segment was just coming on.

The first UFO that was caught on camera looked more like a Frisbee than an alien spacecraft. It was probably a fake. When Jimmy saw the second photo they showed, his eyes widened, and he leaned forward toward the TV. The photo had been sent in by a farmer in a small, rural town called Cragglyville. Despite the picture being taken from far away, there was no mistaking the image: a girl, young, probably no more than ten-years-old, flying high above the earth. The image was too distant to distinguish any of her features, like hair or eye color. But he had a way.

Jimmy slipped on a pair of his boots, the yellow ones that showed the top half of a boy in one spot and the bottom half of the same boy in a different spot. He liked to call them his half-here/half-there boots. He would find out who the girl was and whether she really had powers. If she did, he would go and talk to her, become her friend. After all, kids with powers should stick together.

7

Flying makes you hungry

Upon reaching her house, Nikki was panting, her breathing quick and heavy. Tiny beads of sweat rolled down her cheeks. She had become very tired when they were about halfway home and Mr. Miyagi had practically pulled her the rest of the way. Her watch read five minutes to six, she made it! Trying to get her breathing back to normal, she took in big, slow gulps of air.

She opened the door and walked inside, trying to look as casual as possible. Her dad was sitting in the TV room, having already arrived home from work. Mr. Nickerson worked for a small branch of the national government that was located in Cragglyville, but Nikki didn't know exactly what he did each day. Every time she asked him, her dad would just say, "I mostly just push a bunch of papers around, Nikks. You know, grown up stuff." That was the most she could ever seem to get out of him.

"Hey, Nikks! How was your day, honey?" he asked when she walked in. He turned to look at her and gasped when he saw her face. "Oh my gosh, Nikki, what happened to you?"

Hearing her husband's question, Mrs. Nickerson rushed from the kitchen into the room and said, "Geez, Nikks, did you spend the entire day in the sun?"

Confused by the question and how they had guessed that she was outside all day, Nikki said, "Yes, but how did you know?"

"You're as bright red as a lobster, honey," her mom replied. "You know better than to spend that much time in the sun and not wear sunscreen," she lectured. "What were you doing all day anyway?"

"Ummm, I was just enjoying the day with Mr. Miyagi, but I might have fallen asleep in the grass for a few hours, that's probably why I got burned," Nikki said.

"Well, you really need to be more careful. Tonight you should put some aloe on your face so your skin doesn't peel."

"Okay, Mom, I will," Nikki agreed, trying to avoid any additional questions. "I'm going to use the bathroom before dinner, be right back." She ran up the stairs to the bathroom and closed the door behind her. She looked in the mirror.

Nikki was shocked to see the burnt face looking back at her. She was usually quite pale, with a freckly face, brown eyes, and brown hair. Her white skin and freckles made her prone to sunburn. How could she have been so careless? The power of the sun was probably even stronger because she had been flying high above the trees, with nothing to offer any shade. The next time she flew she would need to use sunscreen and maybe wear a hat too.

She reached in her pocket and extracted the miniature chest. She turned it upside down and around, inspecting it on all sides. She wondered how it could possibly become big again, but decided to deal with it later and shoved it into her pocket. Before returning downstairs, Nikki deposited her backpack, which still held the "flying" gloves, into her room. She hid it under the bed for safekeeping.

At dinner that night, Nikki found that she was starving after her day filled with running, flying, and talking to the strange animal. It had been a mix of something out of Dr. Doolittle and a comic book, and she had loved every minute of it! Her mind wandered to daydreams about using her new powers to help people, like a superhero. She thought about fighting crime like Batman, defending the earth from aliens like Superman did, or even doing simple things like stopping bullies from beating up kids at school.

Nikki was interrupted from her trance when she heard, "Nikki! Chew your food!"

She looked up and realized that while she was thinking about the gloves, she had been shoveling the food into her mouth and her plate was now nearly empty, while her parents still had more than half a plateful each.

"Oops, sorry, Dad. I guess being out in the sun gives me a big appetite."

"That's okay, Nikks. Just go a little slower so you don't choke."

She continued eating, this time at a slower pace, and resumed her daydreaming, while her parents jabbered on about some plan by the local council to build a new road around town to lower the traffic levels. When she finished eating, Nikki pushed back her chair and said she was going to head to bed early.

"What about dessert, Nikki?" her mom asked. "I made a big chocolate cake today."

Anxious to get to her room, Nikki said, "I'm not feeling that great, I think I'll pass, Mom. But thanks," she added.

"Nikki, I have never heard you turn down chocolate before, you must be really sick. It's probably sun poisoning, maybe we should take you to see the doctor tomorrow."

"No, I'm fine, really. I just need to get some sleep. If you put some cake on a plate, I'll take it up with me." Apparently satisfied by Nikki's response, her mom cut a generous slice of cake and Nikki carried it upstairs to her room. Mr. Miyagi followed her, as he always did, but uncharacteristically, Nikki closed her bedroom door before he could get in. She heard him scratching and whining at the door, but she ignored him.

8

Nikki creates a BIG storm

Once in her room, Nikki locked the door to prevent anyone from accidentally discovering her secrets. Adults wouldn't understand this sort of thing, so she wanted to be very careful to hide the gloves from her parents.

Spencer, on the other hand, was a different story. She shared everything with him and this would be no exception. Flipping her phone open, Nikki sent a simple text message to him:

U busy?

Her phone vibrated less than a minute later and she looked at his response.

Yep, eating at GGs, what's up?

"GG" was what Spencer called his grandmother who lived in New York. Whenever he spent the summer with his dad, he would also spend a lot of time with GG. Nikki replied:

Call me ASAP. BIG news!

And seconds later, Spencer responded with:

OK, gimme 1 hr, Popsicle

Nikki laughed to herself. Spencer was always saying weird things and calling her random names like Popsicle or Juicy-Fruit. Most kids at school thought that he was strange, but Nikki loved his quirkiness.

Still smiling, she snapped her phone shut and reached under the bed to retrieve her backpack. Unzipping it, she laid the gloves with the bird picture onto her bed. She looked at them for a few minutes, trying to decide what to do next. Giving in to the temptation, she put them on and pressed her thumb against the bird symbol.

In her mind, a battle commenced between her more responsible half and her adventure-seeking half—almost like the classic angel and devil argument. The "angel" said, "Wait until you're outside, Nikki, you haven't really mastered flying yet." And the "devil" responded, "Don't be such a wimp, flying is fun and you won't get better unless you practice."

The devil has a point, Nikki thought. So she thought hard about her body rising off the floor by a couple of feet. Slam! Her body burst upwards and smashed into the ceiling. Thud! Gravity reclaimed her and she fell through the air, crashing hard onto the floor.

She lay there trying to breathe, the wind knocked out of her lungs from the impact. "Nikki!" she heard her dad yell. "Is everything alright?"

She took three large breaths and then, finding her voice, shouted, "Everything's fine, I just knocked something over!"

Hoping her response would keep her parents from coming up to check on her, Nikki pulled herself up onto her bed. "New rule," she said aloud. "No flying in the house." She slipped the gloves off and placed them next to her, before pulling the baby chest out of her pocket once more. Interested to see what the gloves would look like when they were really small, she used her thumb and index finger to pluck the lid off.

Whack!

Nikki was nearly knocked off her bed from the impact, as the chest magically expanded, reaching full-size in mere seconds. Because it was not sitting securely on the floor when she opened it, the chest teetered on the edge of the bed before toppling over and colliding with the floor, making a loud crash that vibrated through the walls and floorboards.

The sound will definitely get my parents' attention this time, Nikki thought. She hopped off of the bed and tried to flip over the capsized chest, but it was too heavy. Instead, she decided to try to lift the less-heavy lid and slide it back onto the sideways chest. When she reached the lid, she heard someone rattle the doorknob, trying to open her bedroom door. Finding the door locked, the someone knocked hard and demanded, "Nikki, let me in right this instant!" It was her father.

Trying to buy time while she dragged the lid over to the chest, Nikki said, "Just a minute, Dad!"

Reaching the edge of the chest, Nikki heaved and lifted the lid, pushing it with all her might, as she heard her mom say, "I have the key, dear."

The lid snapped into place and the chunky chest disappeared from sight, returning to its miniature form. It was not a moment too soon as she heard the key turn in the lock and the door click open. Her dad's face was red with anger and her mom's brow was wrinkled in concern.

Nikki sat on her bed like she had been there the entire time, and shifted her foot to cover the chest, which was now no bigger than a marble. "What is going on in here?" her dad demanded.

"Nothing, Dad, I was just getting ready for bed and knocked over a lamp. Then when I tried to set it back up, I tripped and fell. I am such a klutz sometimes," Nikki said, laughing at her own expense.

"It sounded like something much bigger than a lamp, Nikki."

"Like what? There is nothing much bigger in here, unless you think I knocked my dresser over. Or maybe it was my bed. Trust me, Dad, it was just the sound being magnified through the house by the old floorboards or something." Nikki impressed even herself with her last lie; it gave some plausibility to her entire story.

Her father didn't seem convinced, however, but seeing that his daughter was uninjured and nothing appeared to be broken, he turned and shepherded his wife out the door. Calling over his shoulder, he said, "Whatever you are doing, just please be careful. And don't lock your door again. Okay, Nikks?"

"Sure, Dad," Nikki replied, thankful that she had been able to talk her way out of trouble, and even more relieved that she had been able to shrink the chest before her parents barged into her room.

As soon as they left, Nikki walked across her room, closed the door, and relocked it, despite her father's clear instructions to the contrary. Whatever punishment she might get for disobeying him would be far better than what could happen if they found the chest or the gloves.

She picked up the toy chest again, but this time she placed it on the floor in the center of the room, away from any furniture. She opened one of her drawers and found a beginner's sewing kit her mom had bought her for Christmas last year, and drew out a long piece of black thread. Using a small knob located on top of the lid, Nikki secured the string to the lid and, while still holding the other end of the thread, she backed away several steps.

Ever so gently, she pulled the end of the string and lifted the lid off the chest. Once the lid was removed, the box's frame burst outwards, and moments later the full-size magical chest stood open in front of her.

Nikki returned the flying gloves to the box and pulled out another pair, one she hadn't tried yet. These gloves were two colors—black on one side and yellow on the other—and had a picture of a lightning bolt on them. Nikki could guess what that meant.

She excitedly pulled on the gloves and crawled onto her bed and over to the window. She concentrated, trying to picture dark clouds rolling in. Within seconds, the previously clear night sky was obscured by black clouds that covered all evidence of the moon and the stars.

Nikki smiled and proceeded to use her mind to open up the clouds and release a torrential downpour. There were deafening roars of thunder and rapid bursts of lightning, followed by a period of hail for good measure.

Nikki was practically giddy with excitement as she watched the fireworks display—*her fireworks display*. After twenty minutes of controlling the weather, Nikki was ready to move on to the next power, so she slipped off the gloves and, instantly, the storm ended and the clouds disappeared, revealing the clear, night sky once more.

She threw the lightning gloves back in the chest and was about to grab another pair, when a large yawn caught her by surprise. She felt drained, a testament to the busy day she'd had, both physically and mentally. She remembered that she had the whole rest of the summer to explore the many powers the gloves could give her.

After returning the lid to the chest, Nikki placed the now-shrunken box under her pillow for safe-keeping, opened the door to let Mr. Miyagi in, and then lay down to sleep.

Her head had barely touched her pillow when her cell phone rang. In all of her excitement she had forgotten about Spencer. Nikki accepted the call and answered, "Hi, Spence, you are never gonna believe what I did today."

Spencer was silent as Nikki told him about following the Weeble along the secret path into the forest and how she had been given the magical treasure chest as a gift. She described all of the different kinds of gloves and the powers she had discovered so far. When she finished, Spencer exclaimed, "Wow, Nikky-Nacky! You might be the luckiest kid in the world! You found powergloves! Kazaa!"

"What do you mean?" Nikki asked.

"You found a bunch of gloves that have different powers, they should be called powergloves! Hoot hoot!" he practically shouted. Spencer was talking faster and faster and making more and more strange noises the more excited he got.

Nikki thought about it for a minute. *Powergloves.* It had a nice ring to it. She liked it. "Powergloves! That's awesome!"

"And now you have to think about coming up with a superhero name, something with powergloves in the name. It's like *Ghostbusters*, they put ghost in their name and it worked perfectly."

"Whoa, hold on a minute, Spence. I haven't done anything yet. I'm no superhero!"

"Well, what are you planning on doing with the powergloves, Cocoa-Puff? You can't have such a power and not use it for good. Remember what Spiderman's uncle said? 'With great power comes great responsibility.'"

"But I haven't even really learned how to use them yet and there are a lot of gloves I haven't even tried yet. But it would be cool to have another name. I'm really tired of being called 'Nikk-Nick' at school."

"That's the spirit," Spencer said. He started humming in the background. As usual, Spencer was thinking. After a minute, he said, "I got it! What about Nikki Powergloves? Shazaam!"

As soon as Nikki heard the words roll off of Spencer's tongue, she fell in love with them. "I love it, Spence! I would get to keep my first name, which I like, and change my annoying last name to something way cooler. Nikki Powergloves it is!"

And just like that, a hero was born, Nikki Powergloves. The only problem was that she hadn't done anything heroic yet.

9

The dangers of powers

After getting off the phone with Spencer, Nikki fell into a restless sleep, her dreams filled with daring rescues and captured bank robbers. All of these feats were accomplished by a new child hero, Nikki Powergloves.

Nikki knew that she would need to practice with her new powers before she could become a hero, but after talking to Spencer, she really felt like she could do it. Her boring life had become filled with endless possibilities.

Upon wakening on Wednesday morning, she hopped out of bed, did her morning chores in record time, pocketed the chest full of gloves, and trotted downstairs, ready for adventure.

Her dad would typically have left for work by now, but today he was downstairs in front of the TV. "Good morning, Dad," Nikki chirped.

"Oh, hey, Nikks," he said. "That was some strange weather we had last night, wasn't it?"

Nikki's stomach lurched. She had forgotten about the storm that *she* had caused the previous night. "Really? What happened? I think I must have slept right through it."

"You must have been really tired; the thunder was remarkably loud. It was a perfectly clear night and then, out of the blue, a massive thunder and lightning storm hit. Not even the meteorologists saw it coming. It did a lot of damage around town."

Damage? *Oh no*, Nikki thought. She listened to what the TV reporter was saying:

"Reports are coming in from all around town about serious flooding causing damage to crops and houses, as well as power lines that are down due to lightning strikes. The repair and cleanup efforts will take a few weeks and the damage done to many of the crop fields will be irreparable. The freak storm has become an anomaly that will likely stump experts around the region for years to come. This is Susan Davis, reporting from Channel 7 news."

Her dad clicked off the TV. Nikki was not feeling so adventurous anymore—in fact, she was turning a bit green.

Noticing his daughter's discomfort, Mr. Nickerson said, "Nikki, you don't look too good, are you feeling okay?"

Nikki decided that some honesty was warranted in this situation. "Not really, Dad. I think I may just go back to bed for a while longer, I didn't sleep too well last night."

"Okay, honey. I hope you feel better soon," her dad said, kissing her on the forehead. "See you tonight."

Feeling her stomach lurch again, Nikki ran upstairs and into the bathroom. She slammed the door, fell to her hands and knees, and leaned over the rim of the toilet. Peering into the toilet water, she saw herself, Nikki Powergloves. Not as a hero, but as a criminal. That's when she barfed.

She heard footsteps shuffling up the stairs. Probably her mom. Her guess was confirmed when the bathroom door opened without a knock. "Nikki, are you okay, sweetie?" her mom asked.

"Not really, Mom," Nikki croaked, still hanging over the toilet.

Springing into action, her mom found a washcloth and wet it. She helped her daughter wipe her mouth and get to her feet. After giving her a drink of water, she prepared her toothbrush for her. Nikki felt a lot better once her mouth was clean again, but she still had a horrible feeling in the pit of her stomach.

"You still don't look too good, Nikki, you should probably just rest today," her mom said, helping her to her bedroom. Nikki didn't argue and collapsed in a heap on her bed, allowing her mom to tuck her in. Mrs. Nickerson left to run some errands and told her to try to get some rest.

Nikki wanted to sleep to get her mind off of what the news reporter had said, but the words kept streaming through her head: "…flooding causing damage to crops and houses… power lines down due to lightning strikes…repair and cleanup efforts will take weeks…damage to crop fields will be irreparable…"

She needed someone to talk to and the only one who knew her secret was Spencer, so she called him.

He answered on the first ring. "Hey, Nikki Powergloves!" he answered. "Have you done anything hero-like today?"

She groaned at the question. "Listen, Spence. I think I'm just going to get rid of the gloves—maybe burn them or something—they are really, really dangerous."

"What happened?" he asked.

"I did something bad with them, Spencer, and I don't know what to do."

"Tell me, Dust-Devil, I can help you figure it out."

She told him that the thunderstorm she had created the previous night had been way too strong and that it had caused a lot of destruction.

"Wow, I'm just looking at the local news on my iPad now, you really tore the place up! Those were some serious shenanigans. Wheeeee!" Spencer said. Despite how bad she was feeling, Nikki couldn't help but smile. Spencer was the only kid she knew who used the word 'shenanigans' regularly. Spencer was also the only kid in their class who had an iPad. He even took it to school and used it to take notes during class. Spencer let her use it whenever she wanted to. Having a genius as a best friend had its perks.

Spencer was "diagnosed as a genius" as he liked to say, when he was only six years old. After consistently outperforming his classmates in nearly every school subject, his teacher had asked his mom if he could take a test designed by a group called Mensa. It was kind of a club for really smart people. Mrs. Quick agreed and he took the test. Spencer had told Nikki all about it. They made him look at shapes and fit them together and do mazes and other fun puzzles. He really enjoyed it. And at the end of it all the Mensa people told him he had an IQ of around 160 and that he was a genius. They recommended all sorts of special schooling where he could be around other kids "like him." Spencer had told his mom that he liked his school and wanted to stay. Treating him like an adult, she let him make the decision. Nikki remembered the day he had told her all of this. When he got to the part about being asked to switch schools, she started crying. She had said, "Don't leave me, Spence. Please, you're my best friend." He just smiled and put his arm around her. "Don't worry, Nikks. I'll never leave you," he had replied. Nikki remembered being so relieved that he had decided to stay. Her best friend, the genius.

Getting back to business, Nikki said, "You're not helping, Spence. You told me I'm supposed to be a hero, but all I am is one of the bad guys. That's why I need to get rid of these gloves."

"No, do *not* do anything, Nikki. There is a way to fix all of this, I know it. But we are going to need the powergloves to help us do it. Look, I was talking to my dad last night, and he is pretty busy and I'm kind of just getting in the way, so we both agreed to cut my visit short this year, and I can come back for Thanksgiving or Christmas or something. I'm going to fly back tomorrow, so just hang on until then. Okay, Cheese-Doodle?"

"No promises, but I will try. Thanks, Spencer."

"Roger that. See you tomorrow."

They hung up and Nikki took a deep breath. She felt better knowing that Spencer would be there to help her with her problem. She had felt so alone watching the news and not being able to tell her parents that she had caused the storm, but with Spence there, at least she would have a friend and an ally. Soon she managed to drift off into a dreamless sleep with the treasure chest full of powergloves tucked deep in the pocket of her shorts.

10

The gorilla photographer

When Nikki awoke she was sweating. Not because she was sick, but because it was really hot in her room, and she was under the covers. The sun was streaming through the window next to her bed. *What time is it?* she wondered. She looked at the clock on the bedside table: two o'clock in the afternoon.

She ripped off her comforter and sighed as air, albeit hot air, rushed over her arms and legs. She heard heavy breathing and saw that Mr. Miyagi had decided to join her for an afternoon nap—he was curled up on the rug next to her bed.

Her stomach hurt, not because she was still sick from the morning's events, but because she was famished. Having not eaten breakfast, or lunch for that matter, her tummy was angry with her and growled and groaned, causing a dull ache in her gut.

Nikki slipped out of bed, careful not to disturb her peaceful-looking dog, and dragged herself downstairs, where her mom was in the midst of baking something. The aroma filled the entire downstairs and as soon as it hit Nikki's nostrils she began craving the source of the wonderful smell. There was no doubt in her mind: it was apple pie!

When she entered the kitchen, her mom asked, "Are you feeling any better, honey?"

Nikki nodded, "A little bit, thanks, Mom. What are you baking?" she asked, already knowing the answer.

"I've already baked one apple pie and I have another in the oven," she answered. "Farmer Miller brought apples over today, freshly picked from his orchard. Considering your stomach issues, I think you better wait a couple of days before having any though. You should just stick with chicken soup and Jell-O for now."

A look of terror crossed Nikki's face. "Please, please, Mom. I swear I am well now, it was just a quick stomach thing and I am completely fine, I promise!"

"Hmmm," her mom mused. "Well, I suppose we can try giving you a small piece and if you can keep that down we can try a bigger one. But I want you to eat some chicken soup too. Deal?"

A big smile spread across Nikki's face. "Sure, Mom, can I have the pie now?" she asked, rubbing her hands together. Her mom cut her a thin slice that Nikki thought was ridiculously small, but she didn't argue. She was happy to get any at all. She devoured it in seconds and slurped up the soup her mom had prepared.

An hour later, when she had proven that her stomach could handle solid food, her mom allowed her to have a normal-sized piece of pie. She devoured the sweet treat and then lay on the couch to watch TV. The third *Spiderman* movie was playing, starring Toby McGuire. She watched him make mistakes and occasionally screw things up, but eventually save the day in the end, a true hero.

She thought about her own mistakes and realized that although she had been very careless with her powers, she had never intended to hurt anyone. *Having good intentions—that is important*, she thought. As long as she intended to do good, and was more careful in the future, maybe she *could* still be a superhero.

Nikki's mom walked into the room. "Are you feeling any better, honey?" she asked.

"I think so," Nikki replied. She considered whether to open up to her mother. Her mom had always been honest with her and she usually felt better when she talked to her. She decided to give it a try. "I have just been feeling a bit sad lately."

"Aww, honey. What's eating you?"

"Do you think I'm a good person?"

Mrs. Nickerson's brow furrowed. "Now why would you ask a silly question like that?"

"Well, sometimes I want to do the right thing, but when I try to do it everything turns out all wrong."

"It might be easier for me to help if you could give me an example," her mom said.

"I don't really have one."

"Okay, I'll do my best with just your general question. You asked if I think you're a good person and my answer is that I think you are one of the best people I know. Let me give you an example. If Spencer asked you for help with his homework, wouldn't you help him?"

Nikki thought about this for a moment and then replied, "Yes, but Spencer never asks for help with his homework!"

Nikki's mom laughed. "Good point, bad example. But you *would* help him if he asked, that's the important thing. Let me see if I can come up with a better example. Ahh, I've got it. Remember when Grandpa Bernard needed help with his yard?"

Nikki's eyes lit up. "Yeah! After Grandma died, he had trouble keeping it pretty. So I helped him pull out all the weeds and spread the mulch." Nikki's eyes clouded. "Do you miss Grandpa, Mom?"

She nodded.

"Me, too," Nikki said. Memories flooded Nikki's mind. Her grandpa had been one of the most important people in her life, almost like a mentor. He lived in Cragglyville his entire life and had served on the police force for more than forty years. Sometimes he would let her ride in his police car, and he would stop to buy her candies from the corner store. If she asked, he would tell her stories about his life. His father, her great-grandfather, had been one of the original town planners for Cragglyville. Grandpa Bernard used to say, "You look just like my father, Francis Nickerson, God bless his soul. You are a lot like him too, Nikki. He was brave, a good man. He would be very proud to have you as his great-granddaughter."

Nikki smiled at the memories.

"What?" her mom asked.

"I was just thinking about Grandpa."

Mrs. Nickerson nodded. "He would have said you are a good person, too."

"Thanks, Mom."

Nikki glanced toward the TV and noticed that it was still on, but that she had turned the volume to mute. The news had come on and the top story was a strange one. The live picture showed a gorilla jumping up and down on the steps outside Town Hall. Every couple of seconds, the beast would stomp one of its feet and the stone steps would smash and crumble into pieces from the force. Nikki was about to ask her mom where the gorilla could have come from, when the camera zoomed in on the animal's face.

"Heyyy, that's not a real gorilla," Nikki said.

"No, it appears to be someone dressed up like one. That is really sad that someone would do that. Those steps are a hundred years old and considered to be a historic landmark. Do you remember whose name is on them?"

Nikki thought hard and then it hit her. "Great-Grandpa Francis!" she yelped.

"That's right. As one of the twelve town planners, his name is carved into the steps of Town Hall."

Nikki remembered what her mom had said about Grandpa Bernard: *He would have said you were a good person, too.* Now was her chance to prove it.

She said, "Mom, I'm going to go outside to play for a while."

"Are you sure you feel well enough?"

"Yes, I'm okay now."

"Okay, sweetie. Be careful and come home in time for dinner."

"I will, Mom." Before leaving the house, she darted down the steps to the basement. There was a large storage closet where the Nickerson's kept holiday decorations and other items that were only used at particular times during the year. It was also where they kept old Halloween costumes. Nikki rummaged through the box marked "Ghosts 'n Things," and found what she was looking for—what she liked to call her *Old Man Mask*. The mask was in the form of a wrinkly, warty, hairy, old man's face. Nikki had worn the mask for Halloween a year earlier. Now, it would hide her true identity just in case someone saw her using her superpowers.

She donned the mask and opened her treasure chest, quickly slipping on her sky blue flying gloves, so she could get into town quickly. She raced out the basement door and into the sunshine. Once she was sure no one was looking, Nikki took off into the air and flew in the direction of Town Hall. The wind whipped through her hair as she flew. The sun warmed her face underneath the mask. In less than a minute she could see the building. A crowd was gathering to watch the chaos on the steps. The gorilla-imposter continued its destructive dance and Nikki could see that more than half the steps had been smashed to bits. Police had cordoned off the area, but seemed hesitant to approach the lunatic. She had to do something.

Just when Nikki was considering diving toward the hairy vandal, the beast cocked its head upwards and looked at her. Undaunted, she raced toward it, landing a few paces away.

"Why are you doing this?" she asked.

Instead of answering her, the gorilla placed a hand into a hidden pocket and pulled out a small, metal rectangle. "It has a gun!" someone yelled from the crowd. But Nikki could tell that it wasn't a gun. It was just a camera. The beast pointed it at Nikki, and with a blinding flash, snapped a photo of her. Less than a second later, the person in the gorilla suit vanished into thin air.

11

I know your secret

As soon as the "gorilla" had disappeared, Nikki flew away from the town. She saw at least a dozen flashes of light from bystanders' cameras as she took off. She wasn't worried about being caught on camera, because she was wearing the mask. She was much more worried about who the mysterious vanishing gorilla was.

Her dad had arrived home while she was away, and now both her parents were watching the news, which was flipping between photos of the destruction at Town Hall and Nikki standing across from the gorilla. A couple of reporters were analyzing the events and arguing about the true identity of the masked perpetrators.

"Hi," Nikki said. Her parents were clearly shocked by the news story, as they barely noticed her arrival. "I'm going to check my e-mail," Nikki hollered over her shoulder as she bounded up the stairs.

She heard her mom say, "Okay, dinner in a half-hour."

Hoping to talk to Spencer, she logged onto the internet using the laptop her parents had given her for her 9th birthday. Nikki signed into her instant messenger, or IM, and sent Spencer a short message.

"Hi," she said. Spencer was nearly always logged onto IM when he wasn't with Nikki, so he responded immediately. Their conversation went like this:

SpicNSpence29: hi there, snickerdoodle
NikkNack14: bad news
SpicNSpence29: what?
NikkNack14: check Cragglyville news
SpicNSpence29: wow! is that u with the old man mask?
NikkNack14: yep
SpicNSpence29: who's the gorilla?
NikkNack14: no idea, but can't be up 2 any good. he took my picture
SpicNSpence29: why would he do that?
NikkNack14: i dunno…i am scared. he is strong, destroyed the stone steps
SpicNSpence29: don't worry, i will b home soon. geronimo!
NikkNack14: can't wait 2 see u
SpicNSpence29: u too, c u later alligator
NikkNack14: ttyl

Nikki was about to log off her IM when she received another message, but this one was not from Spencer. It was from JimJim1212 and it read, "Hello, Nikki. I know your secret." Her heart stopped beating for a second and then, panicking, Nikki tapped the log out button and exited instant messenger.

She sat there for a second, trying to breathe. How could someone have found out her secret identity already? And how could they have sent her a message? She had her IM security settings set up so that only people on her "Friends List" could send her a message. And JimJim1212 was definitely not on her list.

She logged into her e-mail account and a notification popped up: "You Have No New Messages." To double-check, she clicked on

"Send/Receive Messages" and sure enough, a new e-mail popped up from JimJim1212@slipperyslope.com. It read:

"Dear Nikki,

I know that you and your friend, Spencer, have been keeping a secret. I know who you are and I want to meet you. I promise I won't tell anyone about you, because I understand how you feel. I have a secret too.

Jimmy"

She snapped her laptop lid shut. *Who is Jimmy?* she asked herself. Was he the gorilla? She needed to find out, and soon. But this was a complicated matter that would require Spencer's help. It would have to wait until tomorrow.

12

Destroying things is fun

Jimmy looked at the crumpled up gorilla suit and laughed. No wonder he had been given special powers. He was way smarter than most kids. Not only had he protected his identity and had a little fun, but he had gathered enough information to track down the girl who could fly. *Nikki Nickerson, what a name,* he thought. He couldn't wait for her to respond to his e-mail, so that they could become friends and start having fun together.

Destroying things was fun. At first he had tried to use his powers to do good things, like the superheroes in comic books. One of Jimmy's powers was finding people. One time, he tried to use his power to help an adopted boy at school find his real parents. He found them, but they didn't even want to talk to the kid. They yelled at Jimmy for contacting them. When he told the boy that his parents didn't want to see him, the boy flipped out and yelled at Jimmy, too!

Eventually he had grown tired of being underappreciated and decided that if people were going to be mad at him anyway, he might as well have some fun with it. That's when he started destroying things. He started small, using his ability to move things with his mind to remove satellite dishes from houses and bushes from people's yards. But eventually he grew tired of that too, so he started using his computer-hacking skills to hack into secure websites and break computer systems. All made possible by the boots he had found.

At night he used to cry himself to sleep because he had no friends, but destroying things always made him feel better. But now, finally, he had found someone who was like him. Someone who had powers. They would surely become best friends. And then they could destroy stuff together. He smiled at the thought and checked his e-mail one more time before going to sleep.

13

Spencer gets a shock (of the electrical variety)

She watched in horror as lightning bolt after lightning bolt struck an old farmhouse, tearing it apart bit by bit. Splinters of wood sprayed through the air, shingles dropped to the ground like dead birds, and windows cracked down the center. She felt someone shaking her while she screamed in fear.

Nikki awoke with a start and the terrors of her nightmare began to fade like a distant memory. Someone *was* shaking her. It was just her mom.

"Nikki, Nikki," she cooed, "It was just a bad dream, honey."

Nikki looked at her mom and smiled. "I'm okay, Mom. I don't remember it already."

"That's good, you had better get dressed though. You have a visitor."

"Spencer!" Nikki exclaimed.

Her mom smiled and left her to get ready.

Nikki hurriedly threw on a pair of comfortable denim shorts and a loose fitting t-shirt. She remembered to pocket the magical chest before running down the stairs. Spencer was waiting for her on the couch, sipping an orange juice and chatting with her mom as if they were best friends, rather than he and Nikki.

"So, Mrs. Nickerson," Spencer was saying when Nikki walked in, "how is chess club? Have you moved up any levels?" he asked her. Spencer sounded very adult.

"Since we had our last match, Spence, I think I've plateaued," her mom answered.

"We'll have to play again soon; I can give you a few pointers that I've picked up at school." Spencer was a member of the chess club at school and sometimes he played with Mrs. Nickerson when he spent the day at their house. Nikki wondered to herself how she had become friends with someone so nerdy when she was so cool? She chuckled at her joke, knowing full well that she was every bit as dorky as Spencer was—that was one of the main reasons they got along so well.

"Welcome back, Spence!" Nikki interrupted.

"Hey, Freckle-Face, did you miss me?" he replied. He was wearing the crooked grin that made Nikki so happy every time she saw him. His braces further accentuated his toothy smile; the orthodontist had only put the metal teeth straighteners on Spencer's teeth a couple of months earlier and Nikki was still getting used to them. His dirty blond hair was messy, like he had just woken up, which apparently he had, sleeping most of the plane ride home. His face was covered in freckles, like hers, just another thing to add to the list of things that they had in common. He was nearly half-a-foot shorter than she was, and about 15 pounds lighter. Between his small stature and glasses, he gave the bullies at school plenty of ammunition to pick on him, but it never seemed to bother him.

"Who you callin' Freckle-Face? Your face is even frecklier than mine! And you were only gone a week, Spence, I was fully prepared for a full month Spencer-free," she said, laughing.

"Well, I'm sure you both have enough to catch up on, so I'll leave you to it," Mrs. Nickerson said, standing up to leave.

"Thanks for the OJ," Spencer said politely.

"You're very welcome, Spencer," she replied. "I'm heading to arts and crafts now, please leave me a note if you decide to go anywhere."

"No problem, Mom, see you later," Nikki said with a wave.

As soon as her mom closed the front door, Spencer looked at her seriously and said, "Show me."

"First, I need to show you an e-mail I got."

Spencer looked at her curiously and then followed her up the stairs. She opened her laptop and showed him the message from Jimmy.

"What do you make of it?" she asked.

"Probably just some goofball-nutcase throwing darts at a board. I wouldn't be surprised if he e-mailed every kid that goes to our school, hoping the right one would get spooked and tell him the truth. I wouldn't even respond."

"I think I need to, even if only to deny it. If I don't respond, I will appear guilty." Nikki realized that she was thinking and talking like a common criminal. She was supposed to be a hero!

"I see your point, Cheerio," Spencer said.

Nikki drafted a simple e-mail, the wording of which they both agreed on. They used a thesaurus to spice it up a little with adult-sounding words. She held her breath and pressed send. Her message read:

"Dearest Jimmy,

I have no idea what you are talking about. Unless you have corroborating evidence for your claims, I suggest you refrain from e-mailing me again.

Ms. Nickerson

PS- Are you the gorilla?"

Ten minutes later they received a response from Jimmy:

"Ms. Nickerson,

I have conducted a simple height and weight analysis from the photo I took. I have also used picture-zoom technology to detect subtle features of the masked girl who flew into town. The result of my work is that I have determined with 99% certainty that you are, in fact, the girl who can fly.

Jimmy

PS- Have you seen any Weebles lately?"

Once finished reading the e-mail, they looked at each other with narrowed eyes. Spencer said, "He seems legit and like he knows what he's talking about."

"I agree. He knows that I saw a Weeble, which I don't even think is a real creature. How could he know that?"

Spencer hummed to himself, puzzling over her last question. "There are only two possibilities, Lucky-Ducky. One, he followed you down the path that day and spied on you while you talked to the Weeble, or two, he has also seen a Weeble."

Nikki's head was spinning. "Spencer, it can't be the first option because Mr. Miyagi was with me the whole time. He has a nose like a bloodhound and would have been barking his head off if he smelled someone hiding in the bushes. That means this Jimmy character has seen a Weeble too. But how could he?"

"He might be asking the same thing about you, Nikki. What if he was led down a secret path, to a secret clearing, talked to a Weeble, and was given a treasure chest, just like you?"

"You think that's possible?"

"Sure, why not? It happened to you, didn't it?"

"I guess so. I just wouldn't expect something like this to happen to two kids. It is crazy enough that it happened to me. Wouldn't we have seen something on the news about a child superhero in some other town?"

"Not necessarily. Do you want people to know about your powers? If he was scared he might have decided to keep his powers a secret, just like you." Spencer seemed to have an answer for everything.

"Do you think I should meet him?"

"Not yet. I think we should do some research first, to see if we can find out who we're dealing with." Spencer grabbed Nikki's laptop and typed an e-mail back to Jimmy:

"Jimmy,

I believe you. Let me think about whether I want to meet. I know you have probably seen a Weeble and have powers of your own. I'll contact you soon.

Nikki"

Satisfied with his work, Spencer sent the e-mail and then typed "mischief vandalism" into the Google search bar. He clicked "Search" and the results were instantaneous. The top ten results were all related articles about a vandalism epidemic in San Francisco. The "acts of mischief," as the article called them, were all unexplained and all likely caused by kids with too much time on their hands. The article went on to say that the vandalism seemed to be getting worse and that the latest act, "the complete disruption of the city government's cyber-network by hackers," was an outrage to the city and the perpetrators needed to be brought to justice.

The article also explained that it was clear that all of the acts of vandalism and cyber-vandalism were linked, because the kid left a calling card at each site that said, "Brought to you by Jimmy, Boy Wonder!" When the government computers were hacked, the same message was left as the screensaver on all government employees' computers.

"It's him!" Nikki practically screamed.

"Checkmate," Spencer said with a sly grin.

"But how did you know?" Nikki asked.

"I didn't know anything. I just guessed. Given the tone of his e-mails, I could tell he was up to no good. For every hero, there's a villain."

"You think he's my villain?" Nikki asked, looking worried.

"I dunno, maybe. One thing's for sure: I would be very careful anytime you make a public appearance. I have a feeling Jimmy will be looking to embarrass you in front of a crowd."

"Maybe I should just forget the whole thing with the gloves and put them back where I found them. I don't know how to be a hero anyway."

"C'mon, Powder-Puff. I think you know how to be a hero better than most people. And anyway, if you don't stand up to Jimmy, who will?"

Nikki cringed. It was a lot to handle for a nine-year-old girl.

"Okay, I'll think about it. But first, let me show you what I can do."

Without another word, Nikki grabbed his hand and led him back downstairs, through the kitchen and out the door into the backyard. The Nickerson's backyard was surrounded by a high fence to allow Mr. Miyagi to do his business each day without anyone watching him, as well as to prevent him from running away. Her dog was waiting and ran up to greet them. He especially liked Spencer, who was always willing to take a few minutes to give him a good scratching.

Spencer crouched and used one hand to rub him behind the ears while Mr. Miyagi licked his other hand in a show of affection. Only distracted for a moment, Spencer stood up when Nikki reached in her pocket and pulled out the small box.

"That's it?" Spencer asked, looking confused.

"Yep," Nikki said, enjoying seeing her friend's reaction. "Now watch this." She placed the box on the grass and carried the attached string a few feet back. "Hold Mr. Miyagi," she instructed.

As she had done in her bedroom, Nikki gave the thread a gentle but firm pull, and the lid popped off. Magically, the chest doubled in size. Then it doubled again, and again, until it had reached its full size.

"Incredible, it's cooler than the first time Luke Skywalker used his light sword in *Star Wars*," Spencer whispered.

"That's nothing compared to what's inside." Spencer followed Nikki over to the chest and watched as she pulled out the black and yellow gloves with the lightning bolt symbol. "These are the ones I accidentally caused the flooding with." In succession, she showed him the white, red, and light blue gloves and explained what she could do with them. Spencer listened in fascination.

"What about the others?" Spencer asked, gazing at the remaining gloves in the chest.

"I haven't gotten that far yet," Nikki said. "I was too freaked out after the thunderstorm."

Always organized, Spencer reached in his pocket and pulled out a folded piece of paper and a pencil. "We need to handle this logically. The first thing we should do is try them all and create a list."

"I'm not sure that's such a good idea," Nikki replied.

Spencer looked her in the eyes and said, "Pizza-Hut, I know you're scared, but trust me on this, we *will* get through this together. The best way to figure out whether we can do any good is to first try to understand what we are working with."

Nikki thought about it and nodded her head. She knew her friend was right. Being a genius, he usually was.

Knowing they would only have two hours until her mom returned from her Thursday club, they decided to go somewhere more private. After making the chest shrink again—much to Spencer's amazement—Nikki scrawled a quick note to her mom that said:

Went outside with Spencer, going to enjoy the nice day. Don't worry, I wore sunscreen this time. Be back for dinner.

They left the house and headed for the Miller's farm. There was a secret spot on the outskirts of the forest, where there was a thick, circular patch of trees. The trees were surrounded by rosebushes making it seemingly impossible to penetrate; however, Nikki and Spencer had found a way.

There was a particularly low hanging branch that extended out over the thorny rosebushes. While both of them were too short to reach it on their own, they had found a small tree stump they could roll underneath and use as a step to grab hold of the branch. By pulling themselves up, they could work their way along the branch and climb down once they were past the roses.

The first time they did this, they were astonished to find that the center of the patch of trees was mostly empty, with only the tree trunks standing like sentries around the border. The tall trees provided a thick canopy of protection from both rain and sun, and also gave them privacy from any spying eyes that might be passing by.

Using their usual trick, both Nikki and Spencer made it safely into the space they liked to refer to as simply, *The Clubhouse*.

Once inside, Spencer took control of the situation. "Okay, first I would like you to show me the powers you get from the four gloves you already tried. That way, I will have as much information as you do and we can move forward from there."

Nikki agreed and decided to go in the same order that she had initially used. White first. She slipped on the snowflake gloves, which fit her perfectly of course, and aimed her finger at a small rock on the ground and thought about how it would look encased in ice. A white stream shot out of the gloves, covering the rock with a thin layer of ice.

Spencer clapped his hands excitedly. "This is the coolest thing ever, Beach-Ball!"

Beaming, Nikki swapped her white gloves for the red ones and proceeded to do her fire trick, melting the ice she had just created. The rock was back to its original form, except a lot hotter. Spencer found this out when he tried to pick it up and burned himself. "Ouch!" he exclaimed

Rolling her eyes, Nikki said, "What did you expect, Spence, that the flames shooting out of my gloves were just a special effect? It's real fire!"

Next up were the light blue gloves. This presented somewhat of a problem, as there wasn't enough open air in the interior of the tree cluster for Nikki to really fly around, like she had earlier in the week. For demonstration purposes, Nikki simply levitated several feet off the ground and told Spencer to trust that she could really fly like a bird.

The amazing anti-gravity feat really captured Spencer's attention, so much that he couldn't help but to ask, "Would you mind if I tried it out?"

Nikki paused for a second and then answered slowly, "I'm not sure that is such a good idea. The gloves were given to me as a gift and they seem to be tailor-made for my hands."

As usual, Spencer had an answer for this. "Hold up your hand." She obeyed and lifted her hand. He put his own hand against hers. They were nearly identical in size. "Are you trying to hog all the fun for yourself, McNugget?" Spencer accused.

Not wanting to sound selfish, Nikki replied, "No, no, sorry, Spence. Of course you can try if you want to." She handed him the light blue gloves and he proceeded to try to jam his hand into the first one. No matter how hard he tried though, he just couldn't get his hand or even his fingers into it.

After a minute of trying, he handed them back to her and said, "It looks like they are even more magical than we thought. It seems only you can use them." He sounded a bit dejected.

Trying to cheer him up, Nikki said, "Just think, what kind of a superhero would I be if someone could just steal my gloves and take all my powers away from me?"

Knowing she had made a good point, Spencer nodded and then got back to business. "Which one is next?"

"The storm ones," Nikki said, pulling out the black and yellow gloves. "But I don't think it's such a good idea to show you, considering the disaster I caused the first time I used them."

Spencer asked, "Well, what did you think about when you used them the first time?"

Nikki thought back to two nights earlier. She was so excited that she might have gotten a little carried away. "I remember thinking about huge, black clouds and buckets of rain. I pictured many bolts of lightning and loud thunder."

Spencer laughed. "I wonder why that caused so much destruction," he said sarcastically.

"Be quiet, Spence," Nikki retorted. But she saw his point. "Okay, okay, I'll give them another try."

Once the gloves were on, she tried her best to think of a tiny raincloud located directly over where they were. She was very careful not to picture any lightning or thunder. They looked up. The sky had darkened over The Clubhouse and a light drizzle careened onto the treetops.

"Amazing! Neek neek! That's even cooler than Harry Potter's ability to talk to snakes!" Spencer said. Smiling, Nikki pulled the gloves off and placed them back in the chest. The rain cloud dissipated.

"Satisfied?" Nikki asked.

"Yep," Spencer answered. "Now we can begin to inventory all of them. Let's start by lining up all of the gloves in the chest so we can see what we're working with." After saying this, Spencer started to reach his hands into the chest. As he did so, there was a blinding light and a searing bolt of electricity. His body convulsed and he was thrown backwards, smashing into a tree trunk and crumpling to the ground.

"Oh my gosh, Spencer!" Nikki yelled, running to where he lay. "Are you okay?"

He rolled over onto his back and looked up at her. "That felt like the time Big Danny rammed me into my locker. It was like Bigfoot gave me a swift kick into a tree."

Nikki laughed, glad that her friend was well enough to make a joke, and offered him a hand to help him to his feet. He accepted it and stood gingerly.

"That is really gonna hurt tomorrow," he said. "It seems that not only can I not put your gloves on, I can't even reach into the chest. It was like a massive electric shock. I still feel a little bit tingly."

"Sorry, Spence. I didn't realize I had such a good security system."

"That's okay, maybe you could just lay them out in the chest and I can peek around you." He seemed afraid to go anywhere near the chest after his last experience with it.

Nikki easily reached into the chest and organized the gloves into matching pairs and then spread them out so that each color was visible, along with the symbol printed on it. Spencer began writing frantically and after a few minutes displayed his inventory. There were three columns, one for glove color, one to describe each drawing, and one to describe the power. His initial notes were:

Powergloves Inventory

Glove Color	Glove Picture	Power
White	Snowflake	Create ice
Red	Flame	Create fire
Light blue	Bird	Fly
Black & yellow	Lightning Bolt	Control the weather
Green	Leaf	?
Purple	Muscly arm	?
Orange	Shoes	?
Gray	No picture	?
Brown	Paw print	?
Pink	Tarot card	?
Gold	Clock	?
Peach	Two identical stick figures	?

"Where should we start?" Spencer asked.

Before Nikki could respond, she heard crazy laughter from above her. She looked up and saw something big and black—it was blocking the few rays of sunlight that had managed to slip through the trees, casting a shadow across her face. With a crack, the black something fell, snapping branches and scraping past leaves, as it hurtled toward them.

"Run, Spence!" she yelled, grabbing his hand and sprinting for cover. She could feel the weight of the falling object bearing down upon them, even though it hadn't reached them yet. When she knew a collision was imminent, Nikki shoved Spencer and then dove after him, landing awkwardly in a jumble of arms and legs on the edge of the clearing. THUD! Whatever had fallen sounded like it had been shoved deep into the dirt.

When they were able to untangle themselves and stand up again, they were shocked to see what lay before them. A giant, black, stone statue of a horse and rider was half-buried in the dirt. The front legs of the horse protruded from the ground while the rider remained fully visible. The statue was chipped and broken, a missing tail here and a missing ear there.

"Arthur Munroe!" Nikki exclaimed.

"Yep," Spencer said.

"You don't think…"

"Yes, I do, Crazy-Horse. I'll give you three guesses as to who did this, but you will only need one."

"Jimmy."

"He's a jerk. That statue means a lot to this town."

Arthur Munroe was the explorer who originally discovered the land that the town was built on. His statue had stood in the Town Center for more than a century. It was the pride of Cragglyville. Jimmy had now personally attacked the town twice: first it was the steps of Town Hall and now it was a historic monument.

"He's a jerk," Spencer repeated.

They heard laughter from above. When she looked up, Nikki had to shield her eyes with a hand, as a ray of light penetrated the foliage. A shadowy form was silhouetted against the sun. *Jimmy*, she thought.

"Get him! Charge!" Spencer yelled.

Nikki nodded and jammed on her flying gloves. Leaping, she shot into the air. As she gave chase, Jimmy used a burst of speed to arc across the sky. Right when she felt like she was gaining on him, he disappeared. Just like before. One moment he was there, and the next he wasn't.

Nikki returned to the ground and in response to Spencer's questioning face, she said, "He got away."

"Darn."

"I don't know if I will ever be able to catch him. Not with that disappearing trick of his. He's going to destroy the whole town!"

Spencer put his arm around her. "No he won't, Gizmo. You'll stop him, I know you will. But he has the advantage of knowing his powers and has probably practiced a lot with them. We just need to learn about your powers as soon as possible, so you'll be ready the next time."

"Okay, I'm ready." Nikki started to move toward the center of the clearing, but stopped when she noticed the statue again. "Uh, what should we do with that?"

"Nothing for now. If we take it back, Jimmy will just steal it again and destroy it more. Plus, it will need quite a bit of repair. Let's just keep working on your powers and we can decide what to do with it later. Which power should we start with?"

14

Nikki licks Spencer's face

"Why don't we just start at the top of your list, which would be green," Nikki suggested. Before Spencer had a chance to answer she grabbed the gloves with the leaf printed on them and slipped them over her hands. "What do you think the leaf means, Spence?"

"It's gotta be the ability to grow things, but I'm not sure where that would really come in handy."

"Okay, let me try." After the storm incident, Nikki wanted to be very careful when trying out any new powers, so she scoured the ground for the smallest plant she could find, a tiny weed with a small yellow flower on it—a dandelion. Pointing her green finger at it, she imagined it growing into a good-sized flower.

To their astonishment, the plant sprouted up, high into the air above their heads. The thin stalk widened to a foot in diameter to support the sunflower-sized flower that now sprouted from its peak.

A look of excitement crossed Spencer's face. "I know how we can use this one! Eek eek eek!" he exclaimed. Nikki waited for him to continue. "What are you most sad about?" Spencer asked cryptically.

Over the last couple of days Nikki had been most sad about the destruction she had accidentally caused to their small town, but she knew that Spencer was getting at something in particular. It hit her like a baseball bat to the side of the head: "The farmers' crops getting destroyed," she declared confidently. "I can use this power to help regrow their vegetables!"

"Bingo," Spencer replied.

Nikki jumped up and down in excitement. "I have to do it now. I have to fix what I did."

"Calm down, Eager-Beaver. It can wait another few hours. We should go through the rest of the gloves and see if there are any others that can help fix things."

Trying to control her excitement, Nikki placed the "growing" gloves back in their spot and replaced them with the next pair on the list, the purple ones, next to which Spencer had written, "muscly arm making a fist."

Nikki decided to take a guess at this power. "I think it must be super-strength," she offered.

"Give it a try," Spencer said.

Nikki looked around for a test subject, but finding none, she pictured herself picking up a certain friend of hers. She walked over to Spencer and lifted him up high above her head like he was made of cotton.

"Hey! Lemme down, Nikks! This isn't funny! Whooooop!"

She lowered him gently to the ground and back onto his feet. He glared at her. "You could have picked up the treasure chest or the statue, you know," he said.

"I totally forgot about them, I swear," Nikki said, laughing. But just for good measure she trotted over to the chest and picked it up with one arm and curled it like a barbell, as if it were no heavier than a feather.

Ignoring Spencer, who was pouting because he'd just been picked up like he was a child, by a girl no less, Nikki snatched the orange gloves from the box and put them on. A crisp drawing of a pair of shoes made it clear what this power would be. Seconds later she was doing laps around Spencer—she was going so fast that the only evidence of her movement was a blur of color that passed by his field of vision every couple of seconds.

After about thirty seconds, Spencer called out, "Okay, Speed-Racer, I think we've figured this one out, too."

As if emerging from a hole in time, Nikki appeared from the blur, her legs slowing to a jog, then to a walk, and finally to a full stop. "That was great, I'm not even tired!" she announced.

"Congratulations," Spencer said. He was clearly beginning to tire of Nikki getting to have all the fun. He wrote something down on his inventory sheet. "Gray is next," he said.

Nikki swapped her orange gloves for the gray ones, and turned her hands over and back a few times, so she could see all sides of them. "I don't see a drawing on these," she said.

"I don't know," Spencer replied, "maybe for these gloves you have to try and imagine a bunch of different things and try to figure it out by trial and error."

"I don't think so…" Nikki trailed off. She looked at the sky. Still looking up, she closed her eyes and tried to imagine nothing at all. Not sure if anything happened, she slowly opened her eyes. Everything appeared to be the same as it had been. Except for one thing. Spencer was looking at her with his mouth open, like he had just seen a ghost.

"Where'd you go, Nikki?" he asked.

Thinking he was playing a joke on her, Nikki replied, "What are you talking about? I'm right here."

Spencer nearly jumped out of his skin at the sound of her voice. "Can I touch your arm?" he asked. *What a weird request*, Nikki thought.

"No, you freak," she said. She was about to hurl another insult at him when she noticed something that didn't make any sense. Looking down, she couldn't see her feet. In fact, she couldn't see any part of herself! "What happened to me, Spence, I'm gone!" she yelled.

"That's what I was trying to tell you, but instead of listening you called me a freak. You've just discovered the power of the gray gloves: invisibility."

Coming to terms with the fact that she couldn't see herself, she decided to have a little fun with it. She snuck around to the back of Spencer and yanked his shorts down to his ankles. Wearing only tighty-whities, Spencer's legs looked even whiter and skinnier than usual, and Nikki let out a loud "Whoop!" and began laughing uncontrollably.

"Nikki!! I can't believe you did that! Areeeebaaa!" Spencer screamed. He tugged his shorts back up and started running around with his arms out, trying to catch his invisible friend. She easily evaded him and soon he became tired and stopped. "Nikki, here I am trying to help you and you keep messing around with me. I seem to remember that just a few days ago you were on the verge of destroying the gloves until somebody talked you out of it."

Feeling bad for what she had done to her friend, Nikki pulled off the gloves and reappeared. "I'm sorry, Spence. You're right, you *have* been here for me and I should be nicer. Let's get through the rest of them and then we can plan our next move."

With both sides declaring a truce, Nikki turned back to the chest and extracted the brown gloves, the ones with the paw print on them. She was particularly interested to test her theory on this pair of gloves. Nikki had been a dog-lover since she was a little girl and having the chance to enter their world, if only for a short time, was more than she could ever hope for.

Concentrating hard, she pictured herself running free, not a care in the world, her floppy ears picking up every sound within a mile of where she was. When Nikki opened her eyes, everything looked different. Instead of looking into Spencer's eyes, her vision fell upon his legs. She looked up to find his face. He seemed like a giant now and he had to reach down to pet her under her chin.

Talking in a baby voice he said, "Now, that's a good girl. Can you do a trick for me, Floppy-Ears? If you're good I'll give you a biscuit!"

Nikki tried to say, "Be quiet, Spence! I'm still a human inside," but all that came out was a low, guttural growl. Spencer jumped back.

"Whoa, Nikki. No need to get angry, I was just kidding around. Anyway, it's hard to talk to you like a human when you look so much like a dog." He looked closer at her paws. "Wow, cool! You still have the gloves on, but they look different, like doggie gloves. They fit you perfectly still. But your clothes disappeared. Hmmm, I wonder if you will be naked when you turn back into a human. I hope not!" Spencer chuckled to himself and Nikki growled again, but then waited for him to continue.

Thinking aloud, Spencer said, "Since you can't ask me any questions, I wonder what I would want to know if I was a dog? Hmmm, I guess I would want to know a bit about my appearance."

Spencer sauntered around her in a circle, like a horse buyer inspecting a prize breed. "Firstly, you seem to be a German shepherd and are quite big, probably about five times the size of Mr. Miyagi. You look almost like a small wolf and I suspect you can run pretty fast if you want to."

Nikki tried to picture what she looked like as Spencer described her. He continued, "Oh, and your breath smells awful, like you've been chowing down on garlic and onions." Spencer grinned his toothy grin.

With Spencer still laughing to himself, Nikki the dog leapt forward and tackled him to the ground, landing hard on top of his chest. She took her long tongue and lapped it across his face a few times, making sure that every bit of it was slimed by her doggie drool.

"Aww, c'mon, Slobber-Lips, I was just joking! Gross!" Spencer wailed, trying to wipe his face with the bottom of his shirt.

Using her paws, Nikki pushed the gloves off and magically morphed back into her natural, human form. She was laughing so hard she was nearly crying. "You should've seen your face, Spence, it was classic!"

When he finished drying his face, he looked at her deviously and said, "You know, Nikki, technically you just kissed me about eight times. I thought we were just friends!"

Before he could even laugh at his own joke, Nikki had slipped on the gloves and changed. But this time she wasn't a dog.

15

Spencer pees his pants, nearly

With a loud roar, the lion pounced on Spencer and proceeded to hold him down with one powerful paw. Spencer let out a high-pitched scream, just like you would expect from a girl. As quickly as she had changed into a lion, Nikki changed back into a girl.

Spencer's face was as white as a ghost and he looked so terrified that for a second Nikki was afraid he might have peed himself. Nikki started to apologize, expecting her friend to be angry with her. "Spence, I'm sorry, I didn't know…"

She was surprised when he cut her off and said, "Awesome! I think you can change into any animal you want to! That's even cooler than Dr. Dolittle being able to talk to animals!"

"Uhh, yeah, I think you're right. Look, I'm sorry, Spence, I really didn't know it would work. I expected to just turn into the dog again."

"That's okay. Of course it was really scary at the time, but I guess I should have known that you wouldn't hurt me. How come your paws didn't tear me to shreds anyway?"

"My claws were retractable," Nikki explained. "I remember having the instinct to keep the claws tucked inside my paws since I knew I was just playing, not attacking."

Spencer laughed. "It felt like an attack to me! Yikes!" They both laughed together and then Spencer said, "You should try turning into other animals so you know what you can and cannot do."

Nikki liked this idea and so, for the next hour, Spencer used the back of the paper to list animals and she tried to transform into them. By the end of the hour, the list looked something like this:

Nikki's Animal Powers

Dog tiger cheetah lion koala ~~antelope~~ ~~bird~~ bear ~~dinosaur~~ chipmunk ~~shark~~ ~~pig~~ ~~fish~~ ~~elephant~~ ~~cow~~ ~~horse~~ raccoon panther cat ~~turtle~~ ~~giraffe~~ monkey ~~snake~~ fox

"Do you see any common themes?" Spencer asked.

"They all have four legs, although monkeys front legs are more like arms," Nikki replied.

"What about warm-blooded? None of the cold-blooded animals like snakes or reptiles worked."

"Yeah, I think you're right. Also, the animal has to have something that resembles a paw; the animals that have hooves like the horses and giraffes didn't work either."

Spencer summarized their findings: "So, it seems like you can basically change into any animal with warm-blood, four legs, and paws. Although I'm not sure it is necessarily defined that specifically, as the monkey seems a bit different."

"Great," Nikki said. "Can we take a break? It's lunch time and I'm starving."

"Sure, Yogi-Bear," Spencer said, opening his bag. "I thought this might take a while so I had my mom pack us a picnic."

A huge smile formed on Nikki's face. "Thanks! I really didn't feel like going all the way home."

They enjoyed delicious peanut-butter and jelly sandwiches, cut diagonally, just the way Nikki liked them. They washed them down with a can of Coke each and chatted as they relaxed in the shade.

Always thinking ahead, Spencer said, "After we're done testing the gloves we have to work on a costume for you."

"Yes, and it needs to hide my true identity. I don't want my mom and dad finding out about any of this."

"At least we have your name figured out. Nikki Powergloves to the rescue!" he shouted.

Nikki giggled. "I hope I'm a good superhero."

"I know you will be. Especially with all the powers you have. I've never heard of a superhero with this many powers before."

"What about a super-villain? Jimmy seems to have lots of powers, too. I mean, you saw the way he was able to fly and drop the statue on us. Plus, with his disappearing and smashing the steps, he seems invincible."

"Don't underestimate yourself, Wonder-Woman. Remember, we know that you have invisibility now, too, so you can sneak up on him. And we still have more gloves to test."

"And I've got the best genius sidekick ever!" Nikki added.

"You mean, you really want me as your sidekick?" Spencer asked uncertainly.

"Of course! You're my best friend and are smarter than anyone I know, even adults."

"Thanks, Nikki."

After finishing their sodas they got back to business. Next on the list were the pink gloves with the tarot card symbol that Nikki had been dying to try out. From her experience, a tarot card meant seeing the future. She pressed her thumb to the symbol and closed her eyes.

She wasn't sure how to imagine herself seeing the future, so she just pictured herself in a dark room with a crystal ball. In her mind, she looked deeply into the glass orb. Visions flashed through her head. She saw she and Spencer starting fifth grade. There was a gang of bullies that were picking on a skinny, nerdy-looking kid. He was new at school. The movie continued and she saw herself spring into action, using her super-strength gloves to fight him.

Everything went dark as the scene changed, and then she saw the bully in the hospital with bandages on his head; she had hurt him pretty badly. The scene changed again and she was in the car with her parents. They pulled into a different school, the sign said: "St. Bernard's Juvenile Academy." *Oh no*, she thought, *I was forced to go to a juvenile delinquent school because I beat up the bully!* "No!" she yelled. "Don't leave me here, I was only trying to help!" Her parents left her at the school and drove away.

Nikki opened her eyes. Spencer was staring at her. He looked alarmed. "What did you see?" he asked. "You were yelling."

"I saw me defending a kid that was getting picked on at school. I used my powergloves. I beat up the bully and they kicked me out of school and sent me to juvie." Nikki said all of this without emotion, in a monotone voice.

"But that can't be true, can it?"

"It has to be, Spence, the gloves have worked so far, so why wouldn't these ones be able to show me the future?"

"Maybe so, but that doesn't mean the future can't be changed. You probably just saw what can happen if you are not careful with the way you use the gloves. Like with what happened with the storm."

Nikki's face brightened. "Do you really think that the future can be changed? I don't want to go to that school, Spence."

"I don't know, but I think there is a way we can test it. I bet you can see any future that you choose. Almost like seeing the trailer for a movie before you go to watch the whole thing. If I plan to do something in the next few minutes, I think you might be able to predict what I will do before I do it."

"Okay, let's try it. Plan to do something and I will try to stop you."

Spencer thought for a minute and then said, "Okay, ready."

Nikki closed her eyes and saw the crystal ball again, but this time, she focused on Spencer and what he might do in the next few minutes. Sure enough, she saw her and Spencer in The Clubhouse. He was standing across from her and they were looking at each other. Suddenly, he ran toward the magic chest and tried to stick his hand inside. Like before, there was an explosion of sparks and he was jolted backwards into the air, like a circus acrobat shot out of a cannon.

She opened her eyes and Spencer was staring at her, just like in her vision. She stared right back at him. As she expected, he tried to make a dash for the chest, but knowing what he would do, Nikki was able to run in front of him and block his way with her arms.

"Awesome! Hallelujah!" Spencer yelled. "That's even cooler than the first time Anakin Skywalker went pod-racing in the new *Star Wars*! You can definitely change the future, Nikki. There's no need to worry about what you saw. When the time comes, you just need to handle the situation differently. Maybe use your ability to change into a bear so you can scare the bully away. No one will even know it was you."

Nikki was relieved to find out that she didn't have to go to juvie. She had heard that only the toughest kids went to school there.

They moved on to the next pair of gloves—the gold ones with a clock on them. Spencer said, "You can probably stop or slow down time, or maybe both."

He had guessed correctly and when Nikki put on the gloves she was able to bring time to a crawl, like she was watching a slow motion replay on TV. The coolest thing though, was that she could still move at her normal speed. They had agreed before the test that Spencer would run laps around the chest so that Nikki could see what it would look like if a bad guy was trying to run from her when she used her gold gloves.

Spencer's running was so slow that she could walk next to him and easily keep up. Nikki could even run circles around him while he was running around in a circle. It was like he was the planet earth circling the sun and she was the moon circling the earth. She could probably circle him 365 times before he could make 1 revolution around the chest.

Eventually she tired of watching him move in slow-mo, so Nikki stopped time altogether. His body was stuck in place, with one foot out in front of the other, in mid-stride. Deciding now was the time to play another joke on her friend, Nikki bent down and tied his shoelaces together. *This is gonna be good*, she thought.

Allowing time to start again and go back to its normal speed, Nikki watched eagerly as Spencer took his next step. His legs locked together as his front foot tried to pull his back foot forward because of the shoelace. He went sprawling head-first onto the ground and rolled a couple of times before coming to a stop in the grass.

"Geez, Spence, what happened?" Nikki asked. "You must have tripped on something."

Spencer looked down at his shoes to find they were shackled together. "Very funny, Geek-Squad. They certainly didn't tie themselves together did they?"

Nikki feigned innocence and said, "I don't know what you mean."

Spencer stood up and brushed himself off. Turning serious, he said, "It was weird, I was moving at normal speed, but I could barely see you. It was like you were moving at the speed of light, flashing in and out of my vision."

"That power will definitely come in handy," Nikki noted.

She swapped the gold ones for the last pair of gloves. They were peach colored, almost exactly the color of her skin, and had pictures of two stick figures drawn on them. The stick figures were identical. "What do you think these gloves do?" she asked Spencer.

"My first guess is that you could clone yourself or something," he said.

Nikki rubbed her hands together. "Oooh, I hope you're right. The only thing better than one Nikki Powergloves, is two Nikki Powergloves."

She imagined that there were two of her, and that she and Nikki number two were standing next to each other. When she opened her eyes, she looked around excitedly, but it was still just she and Spence. "I don't think the power is cloning," she said.

Spencer laughed. "I'm glad, I can barely survive one Nikki's pranks, two would be more than I could handle. Hmmm, what else could it be?"

"What about the power to clone other people?" Nikki suggested.

A look of understanding crossed Spencer's face. "I don't think that's quite right, but you're on the right track. It's not that you can clone yourself or others, but that you can make yourself look like someone else! Yip yip yip!"

"I think you're right, Spence. Unfortunately the only one here is you, and not in a million years would I ever want to look like you," she said with a sly grin.

"Ha…Ha," Spencer said dully. "Just try it, would you?"

Chuckling to herself, Nikki concentrated on transforming into a Spencer look-a-like. She heard Spencer exclaim, "Oh my gosh, Nikki, it's like I have a twin brother!"

She opened her eyes. She was wearing Spencer's clothes and her legs looked funny with tiny little hairs growing on them. "Do I really look like you, Spence?"

"Yep, you're my spitting image. I bet you could even fool my mother. Hey, you know how you're much better in history class than I am? Maybe next year you could take a few of my tests for me, whaddya think?"

"I think that would be considered misuse of my powers and would be inappropriate conduct for a superhero," she replied. "You can take your own tests just like every other kid."

Spencer groaned. "Okay fine, but you can't fault me for trying!"

Nikki ran her tongue along her front teeth; she even had Spencer's braces! "Ewww, having metal in your mouth feels weird!" she said.

"Tell me about it. You're lucky your teeth are straight."

Nikki pulled off the gloves and changed back to her normal self. Returning the last pair of gloves to the chest, she said, "Well, that's it. We've tested them all! That was fun, wasn't it?"

Spencer groaned. "Maybe for you! I've been electrocuted, picked up, nearly smashed by a giant statue, tripped, attacked by a lion, and had my pants pulled down. Not one of my best days!"

"True, but you've also been hired as the genius sidekick for a brand new superhero."

"Good point," Spencer replied.

Spencer made a few more scribbles on the paper and showed the finished product to her. It looked like this:

Powergloves Inventory

Glove Color	Glove Picture	Power
White	Snowflake	Create ice
Red	Flame	Create fire
Light blue	Bird	Fly
Black & yellow	Lightning Bolt	Control the weather
Green	Leaf	Ability to grow plants quickly
Purple	Muscly arm	Super-strength
Orange	Shoes	Super-speed
Gray	No picture	Invisibility
Brown	Paw print	Transform into animals
Pink	Tarot card	See future (and change it)
Gold	Clock	Stop or slow time
Peach	Two identical stick figures	Look like someone

16

Powerbracelets: pretty AND useful

Nikki could see something shiny tucked underneath one of the gloves. She reached in and extracted a simple bracelet. It had a thin, silver band inlaid with a single, blue jewel. The jewel was circular and inside of it, Nikki could see the form of a glove, like one of her powergloves, but clear, absent of any color.

"What do you think it does?" Spencer asked, looking over her shoulder at the bracelet.

"I have no idea. The jewel just shows a picture of a powerglove, which could mean anything really. Maybe when I wear it with the powergloves, it makes the abilities even stronger. I would be afraid to try it though, considering how strong the powers are already."

"Why don't you try it on by itself?"

Tentatively, Nikki slipped the bracelet over her hand and onto her wrist. A perfect fit. It wasn't one of those loose fitting bracelets that some girls liked to let jingle and jangle on their arms; rather, it hugged her arm, with no space between the metal and her skin.

Nothing happened. They waited a few minutes, looking at it expectantly. Still nothing. "Maybe it's just for looks, a symbol of my superhero-ness," Nikki suggested.

"Maybe," Spencer said, "but I think you should leave it on."

"I was planning to," Nikki said.

Spencer helped Nikki replace the lid on the chest and watched in awe as the chest became pocket-size seconds later. Nikki was used to the shrinking and growing chest by now and it had completely lost its novelty for her.

After they dropped from the tree branches safely past the thorny guardians of The Clubhouse, Spencer said, "I don't know why we're walking, you could have just flown us home."

"Don't get lazy on me already, Spence. I'm not gonna be giving you flying rides all over town, you know. The powergloves are strictly to be used for hero activities."

Unexpectedly, the silver on her bracelet turned bright white and the jewel lost all of its blue color, becoming completely clear. Nikki and Spencer gazed down at it in amazement, as the image of the powerglove began to spin faster and faster. As it slowly came to a stop, the image turned green and glowed through the clear crystal.

"Wow," Spencer marveled. "We should have known everything that came out of that chest would be magic. Get out your green gloves."

"Why?" Nikki asked.

"I don't know, but the powerbracelet seems to be telling you to. Maybe you are about to need them."

Nikki re-expanded and opened the chest, sifting through the colored gloves until she found the green ones. After donning them, she looked at Spencer and firmly pressed her thumb into the leaf symbol. This time, both of the gloves sparkled as if they were covered in millions of tiny emeralds, reflecting the rays of the sun in every direction. The gloves glowed brighter and brighter, and then, to Spencer's amazement, Nikki disappeared.

17

Nikki becomes a farmer (minus the overalls)

Nikki had been watching with fascination as her green gloves sparkled with beauty. With a jolt, she was aware that something was different. When she looked up, she was confused. Where was Spencer?

She could tell she was still on a farm, on the side of a barn, but she didn't think it was Farmer Miller's place anymore. How did she get here?

Nikki could hear voices nearby, so she crept toward them and peeked around the corner of the red barn.

"What are we going to do this year, Jerry?" A woman was talking to a man; he was probably her husband.

Her probably-husband responded, "We'll make it through, dear, we always do."

"No, not this year. We could barely pay our bills last year with a full harvest and now look at it," she motioned to the fields. Nikki followed her gesture to see a wide expanse of land. There was something lying on the ground, covering the entire field. "The storm destroyed every single stalk of corn before we could get anything from them. It's too late in the season to plant again. We are going to have to sell the farm, Jerry!"

Jerry the farmer pulled his wife to him and hugged her as she wept.

Nikki felt sick to her stomach. This farmer and his wife had lost their livelihood because of her. She had to do something. The growing gloves! She watched as the couple walked into the house, and then she scurried across the lawn and onto the fields. In order to keep this a secret, she was going to have to work fast.

Nikki went all the way to the furthest corner of the cornfield before closing her eyes and, using every brain cell she had, imagined the corn growing again, into tall, strong stalks. She was careful not to overdo it; she didn't want suspicions to be raised by unbelievably tall cornfields.

Opening her eyes, she almost screamed with happiness when she saw the result. The fallen stalks were lifting themselves up and dusting themselves off, as if they were humans that had fallen over. The bent stalks were magically straightened and then the growing began. The stalks looked like new as they grew taller, and Nikki watched with delight as green ears of corn popped out from every side.

She knew that soon the farmer and his wife would notice that something was different and come running out. Wanting to see their reaction, Nikki ran along the side of the field so she could watch from afar. Sure enough, a few minutes later Nikki observed as the woman opened the door to let their dog out. When she did, she glanced up at the field and nearly keeled over backwards in surprise.

The woman let out a loud "Ooooweee!" and yelled, "Jerry, Jerry, come quick!" The farmer emerged and the two of them ran to the fields. They touched the stalks delicately, as if they were worried that the slightest disturbance might knock the crops over again.

"This is just the miracle we needed, honey. Someone is looking out for us after all. We're going to be just fine," Jerry said, embracing his wife once again. The couple wept tears of joy together and Nikki found herself tearing up just watching them.

Nikki felt good about what she had done, but was careful not to have too much pride, as she knew she had caused their problems in the first place. But she was excited for the next day, when she would be able to try to use her new powers to clean up the rest of the mess she had made. Only then would she be ready to start learning how to become a real hero.

Not knowing exactly where she was, Nikki swapped her green gloves for the light blue flying ones and shot off into the air. The farmer and his wife were too busy counting their blessings to see her rocket upwards and across the sky.

Nikki quickly found her bearings and headed in the direction of her house. She was very careful to stay high enough so that anyone that happened to spot her would mistake her for a bird. She helicopter-landed in her backyard—behind her dad's tool shed—and dialed Spencer's cell number.

"Come to my house right away, Spence. Do I have a story for you," she said.

18

Ponytails: childish hairdo, or hidden identity?

Nikki opened the front door to wait for her friend. Moments later, she saw him dashing down the street. When he arrived at her door he was out of breath.

"C'mon in, Spence! My mom's cooking dinner and she said you can join us if you want to!" She practically shouted, so that her mom could hear what she was saying.

"What happened?" he whispered sharply.

"I'll tell you in a minute," she hissed back. Returning to her loud voice, she asked again, "So, can you stay for dinner?"

Playing the game now, too, Spencer shouted, "I think so, I'll call my mom to ask. Yay!" He called his mom and easily obtained permission to eat at the Nickerson's. Nikki knew that Spence's mom always appreciated a night off from cooking dinner, as her shift at the hospital didn't give her much time for domestic responsibilities.

Nikki liked Spencer's mom. In some ways, she looked up to her too. Janet Quick was a doctor and Nikki knew she liked being able to provide for Spencer, but because of her busy schedule, whenever Nikki ate at Spencer's house it was usually frozen meals, a staple in the Quick household. Nikki liked her mom's home cooking much better.

Nikki ran into the kitchen and informed her mom that Spencer was allowed to stay for dinner. Mrs. Nickerson said, "Well, it's a good thing. I made enough food to feed a small army."

Nikki and Spencer's mouths watered, but they would have to wait to satisfy their hunger. Dinner wouldn't be ready for thirty minutes and besides, Nikki wanted to tell Spencer her latest story. She led him up the stairs to her room, where she told him what had happened.

Spencer listened in awe until she had finished, and then said, "Master-Yoda, you saved the day. I would say you are officially a hero. Zoooom!"

Nikki frowned. "That's like saying someone who robs a bank and then returns the money is a hero," Nikki replied smartly. "It was my storm that destroyed their crops, so I am definitely not a hero for fixing it."

"I guess you're right. Well, in any case, you're headed in the right direction now at least. Once you've made up for all the damage you caused you can start to do real hero things, like dealing with Jimmy. And it seems like that bracelet you're wearing will help you to know when you are needed."

Nikki looked at the magical bracelet thoughtfully. She wondered how often it would burst into light to guide her to her next mission. She thought about all the wonderful adventures she would have. Nikki Nickerson had never been this happy in her entire life.

Spencer snapped her out of her daydreaming by saying, "Earth to Nikki..." He waved his hand across her face.

"What?" Nikki asked.

"Do you want to work on your hero costume?"

Excitedly, Nikki said, "Yes!"

"Okay, I have a lot of experience with this considering the ridiculous number of comic books I have read in my life. The first and most important thing is that you cover your face somehow, so that your true identity can remain a secret. Do you have any masks or should we make one?"

Nikki thought about it for a minute. "I have some old masks from Halloween, but they are all scary looking. I don't think they're what we're looking for. Do I have to wear a mask or is there something else we can do?"

Spencer cocked his head to the side and began to hum to himself, the telltale sign that he was doing some serious thinking. After a few minutes his head jolted up and he exclaimed, "What about your hair?"

Nikki looked confused. "What do you mean, 'my hair'?"

"Okay, picture this. You always wear your hair in a long ponytail, right Goldilocks?"

"Yeah, so what?" she replied, grabbing her ponytail defensively. Nikki had been made fun of a few times for her ponytail. Most of the girls at school thought it looked childish and wore their hair down.

"We could use your ponytail to cover your eyes, like a natural mask. We just have to figure out a way to create eye-holes so you can see."

Nikki loved the idea as soon as she heard it and she even knew how to create the eye-holes. She raised her pointer finger as a sign that Spencer should hold on for a minute, and then ducked down and began rummaging under her bed. Within moments, she found what she was looking for: an old shoebox.

After opening the cardboard box, she plucked out two black, plastic circles. The circles were a few centimeters wide and had an indentation around the entire perimeter, large enough to wrap a ponytail around.

Spencer inspected one of them, "This just might work, Nikki. Where'd you get these anyway?"

"I just found them in the dirt at the park last week. I have no idea what they are, but I brought them home and cleaned them off and stuck them in my shoebox in case I ever needed them."

"It's like fate," Spencer suggested.

Nikki shrugged and said, "Now help me put them in my hair." She re-braided her ponytail, making each crisscross tight enough to hold the plastic discs in place.

Spencer used his finger to burrow two gaps in her ponytail and then inserted the plastic circles into the holes he created. Next, Nikki wrapped the ponytail just above her left ear, around the front part of her head, over the top of her eyes, and behind her right ear. The eyeholes ended up in two completely different spots—one fell just to the right of her left eye on the bridge of her nose and the other barely reached the right corner of her right eye.

"I think it needs some work," Nikki joked.

"I'm not sure I understand what you mean, I think it looks perfect," Spencer joked back. "Although, to be honest, I think you look more like an alien or a monster than a superhero. Here, let me fix it." He adjusted the locations of the holes so they were directly even with her eyes. Nikki used a finger to hold the pony tail behind her right ear. She peered out at Spencer.

"How do I look," she asked.

"Surprisingly, you look kind of dangerous, like Zorro, but we will need to something to hold the ponytail behind your ear."

Nikki had just the solution for this and she used one of her simple hair ties to link the ponytail to her ear. "Okay, so you think I look dangerous, which I guess is a good thing if I am going to be fighting bad guys, but more importantly, do I look like Nikki Nickerson....or Nikki Powergloves?"

"I think you are nearly Nikki Powergloves, but it would help if you had a full costume. We should go shopping tomorrow and find something suitable."

"Sounds great, Spence. Now let's eat," Nikki said. She undid the hair tie and the eye-holes and returned her ponytail to its rightful place on the back of her head. They raced back downstairs.

Dinner was delicious with hot rolls, sweet mashed potatoes, roasted chicken, and apple pie for dessert. The only thing Nikki didn't eat was the fresh corn on the cob, although Spencer more than made up for her by having about five ears.

While they were working on her superhero "mask," Nikki's dad had arrived home. He gave them an update on the destruction around town, beginning with the damage caused by the freak storm. "Most of the farms had some damage to their fields, but Jerry Snyder and his wife were hit the hardest. Their entire cornfield was wiped out. I'm not sure how they will get by, although I heard word that some of the local churches are going to take up a collection this Sunday."

Spencer chimed in, "We should pray for them, maybe a miracle will happen."

Nikki glared at her friend, angry that he had said something that would potentially raise suspicions that they were involved in re-growing the Snyder's field.

Spencer ignored her and continued on. "Mr. Nickerson, is there anyone else that had really bad damage?"

"Besides the destroyed crops around the community, there are a couple of houses up on Chambers Street that had large trees fall across their backyards. They will eventually get around to sawing them up and removing them, but it may take a few weeks."

"Oh, I'm sure it won't take that long," Spencer said with a twinkle in his eye. Nikki continued to frown at him.

Mr. Nickerson said, "And there's the vandalism to deal with. The steps to Town Hall will have to be rebuilt and carved with the town planners names again. And I don't know if you heard, but someone stole Arthur Munroe today."

"The statue?" Nikki asked, keeping her face straight. "How could someone have stolen it?"

"The police are wondering the same thing. Apparently it weighs more than a thousand pounds. And it was stolen in broad daylight so it's surprising there were no witnesses. It's a mystery that may never be solved."

"I hope they catch these criminals," Nikki said.

They finished dinner and Nikki walked Spencer to the door in an attempt to get rid of him before he could make any more stupid comments. As soon as he was gone she sent him a text message:

No more dumb comments, pls

He replied with:

Sorry, got carried away

Nikki snapped her phone shut and went to her room. For the next hour she worked on designing what she wanted her superhero shirt to look like. She wanted it to be simple and comfortable. She couldn't imagine fighting crime wearing some of the tights that comic book heroes tended to wear.

Eventually she got tired and crashed on her bed. Mr. Miyagi hopped up next to her, curling at her feet. Her last thought before she drifted off to sleep was that she couldn't wait to become a true hero the next day.

19

The t-shirt genius

Nikki had agreed to meet Spencer at his house the next morning, so at eight o'clock sharp she rang his doorbell. The door opened and Spencer bounded out yelling, "Bye, Mom, see you tonight."

As usual, Spencer was organized. He had a checklist of the tasks they needed to complete that day. Having him as a sidekick was paying off already. The checklist showed:

1. Finish costume
2. Regrow other damaged crops
3. Remove large trees from yards
4. Get Nikki seen doing something heroic

Nikki frowned when she saw the last item on the list. "Why do we have to do number 4? I thought the whole point was to keep my identity a secret," Nikki said.

"We will. That's what the mask and costume are for. But we do want you to get noticed so that people know who is causing all of the amazing things to happen around town. We want to make sure you are recognized as a hero right away, rather than as a villain or a menace to society. Some of the greatest superheroes were tagged as villains by the media, which made things very hard for them. We want people to like you."

Nikki was reminded of Batman, a superhero who was often treated like a bad guy by the very people he was trying to protect. Nikki *did* want people to like her so she was glad she had Spencer to help her with this.

"Okay, sounds good. But I want to do numbers 2 and 3 before number 1. I want to fix the damage I have caused before I worry about my costume."

"That's fine," Spencer agreed. "You're the Big-Boss-Man! Bling bling!"

"I guess our first stop will be the farms. We should go by each one of them and see if they have any need for our help."

Now that their plan was agreed, the pair took off down the road. As they stopped at each farm, they assessed the damage, made a team decision on whether they needed to do anything, and then Nikki used her green gloves to regrow the damaged crops. Spencer's eyes widened each time he saw Nikki use the power of the green gloves. They were careful to stay out of sight at each farm, especially because Nikki did not have a full costume yet.

By noon, they had finished with the farms and were exhausted from romping around the rural area, where farms were sometimes separated by miles. They stopped in town for some lemonade and a bite to eat before setting their sights on the houses with the fallen trees that Mr. Nickerson had told them about.

They easily located the two houses, as Chambers Street was only two blocks long and came to a dead end. Worried they would get caught, they rang the doorbells of each house to see if anyone was home. After two rings with no answer, they crept between the houses to the backyard. A massive tree had fallen across both backyards and smashed some patio furniture and the fence in between the houses.

"Do you think you can carry that with your super-strength?" Spencer asked, seeming doubtful.

"I'm not sure, but I think the bigger problem will be where to go with it. There's another street behind this one and houses on all sides. I can't exactly run down the street with a tree trunk on my back—at least not until I find a place to put it." Nikki scratched her head.

"Why don't you just fly it out, Chicken-Little?" Spencer suggested.

"Because I don't have my super-strength when I fly. I wouldn't be able to lift it."

Spencer began to hum as he thought about the problem from all angles, much like he did when he was in the middle of a chess match. A thought popped into his head. "Are you sure you can't combine the powergloves?"

Nikki's eyebrows raised and she said, "Uh, I've never really tried it."

"Let's give it a shot. Either try wearing the gloves on top of each other or a different one on each hand and see what happens."

Seeing the merits of this idea, Nikki started to pull out two pairs of gloves, but realized she wouldn't be able to wear them on top of each other; the treasure chest only allowed her to use one pair at the same time. However, she hadn't tried removing a mixed pair. She grabbed one light blue glove for flying and attempted to take out a purple one for strength.

To her delight, she was able to take both colors out. "I think this might work, Spence," she said. She put each of the mismatched gloves on. Next she tried to hover and found she was easily able to escape the pull of gravity and levitate above the ground. She grabbed Spencer and slung him above her head, demonstrating that the strength was there, too.

When she set him back on his feet, he asked, "Do you always have to use me to test that one?"

"Yes," Nikki replied, "and you said I'm the Big-Boss-Man so you have to listen to me." She grinned at him and walked over to the giant tree trunk. She easily picked it up with one hand and curled it a few times to show off for Spencer.

"It seems lifting it won't be a problem," she said. "But not getting caught could be difficult because there are so many houses around here. Who knows who's looking out their window right now and might see a nine-year-old girl fly off with a fifty-foot tall tree?"

Spencer said, "I think it's a risk we have to take. Maybe you should use your ponytail mask to make it harder to identify you. I will leave on foot and walk back to town and meet you at Pete's Diner."

Nikki agreed and Spencer helped her tie her braid into a mask. She gave him a ten-minute head start so that he would be well away from the house before she did her superhero thing. Once she felt it was safe, Nikki grabbed the tree and zoomed off into the sky. She flew as high and as fast as she could, so no one could see her from the ground. Once she was above the clouds, she soared for the center of the forest. She dipped below the clouds and then, flying low, dropped the tree and watched as it crashed amongst the trees, just another fallen tree in the woods.

She met Spencer ten minutes later and said, "The eagle has landed."

He laughed at her cheesy code and congratulated her on a job well done. He looked at the list. "Time to finish your costume," he said.

"I've already drawn up how I want it to look," she replied. Her illustration was simple: a skinny girl with her eyes covered by her own ponytail, wearing a t-shirt, shorts and sneakers. The t-shirt was yellow with a light blue glove on it and "NP" written with the "N" slightly higher than the "P".

"Hmmm," Spencer mused. "I'm not sure if this really does you justice. I've never seen a superhero outfit that is so....well, so boring."

"Good, that's exactly what I'm going for," Nikki said. "I don't want to be all flash and dash. I want to be known as the hero who always does good and helps people. Nothing more and nothing less."

"It's your choice, Nikki, but I think you should get some snazzy tights and make it a little more colorful."

"Maybe later. For now, I'm going to stick with my design." With the matter settled they walked down the street to Flanagan's. Flanagan's was a t-shirt shop. In a small town, people wore a lot of t-shirts and Flanagan's offered them in every color, style, and design you could imagine. They could also do a custom design, which is what Nikki was after.

Nikki stopped outside the store and turned to Spencer, "Okay, when I am spotted flying with this t-shirt on, Mr. Flanagan is obviously going to realize it's the t-shirt that he custom-made and he will likely be interviewed by the newspaper. So, to avoid linking the shirt to me, you are going to have to buy it, and later you can say that a strange girl asked you to buy it for her. You can say that you couldn't see her face, because she was wearing a dark hood or something."

Spencer liked the idea of being interviewed for the news. "Sounds great, I'll do it!" He snatched the drawing from Nikki's hand and ran into the store.

While he was gone, Nikki amused herself by using her shiny powerbracelet to catch the sunlight and reflect it onto various objects—a fire hydrant, a mailbox, her shoes, a passing dog. Just when she was getting really bored of the reflecting sunlight game, Spencer exited the store with a small bag in his hand.

"And?" Nikki asked.

Spencer paused for dramatic effect. "I got it! And it looks much better than I expected it would. Flanagan is a t-shirt genius!" Worried that someone would see them looking at the shirt in such a public place, the pair walked around the corner and behind the Lamplighter Hotel. The parking lot was deserted.

With a grand gesture, Spencer whipped out the shirt. "Ta daaaaa!" he proclaimed.

Nikki frowned. She knew she shouldn't have trusted him with her design. "Go back and fix it," she ordered.

"Aw, c'mon, Fashion-Police. It's much better this way, don't you think?"

"No."

"At least give it a chance, it might grow on you."

Nikki stretched the shirt out wide so she could see the whole thing, and tried to take it all in. Spencer had included her original design, a basic yellow shirt with the light blue glove and "NP" logo, but he had littered the front of the shirt with each of the twelve symbols that were on the powergloves. There was the muscly arm and the lightning bolt and the snowflake and so on. Each symbol was printed in the correct color of the glove that it represented. *It is kinda cool,* she thought.

Not wanting Spencer to know that she was starting to like his design, Nikki said grumpily, "Okay, fine. I'll use it for now, but just on a trial basis."

Spencer grinned, seeing right through her act. "I knew you would like it!"

"I do NOT like it!" Nikki snapped.

"Sure you don't," he replied sarcastically. "But that doesn't matter now. What do we do next?"

Trying to breathe to calm down, Nikki replied, "I need new pairs of shorts and shoes, ones my parents have not seen."

They left the parking lot and walked down the street, window-shopping the handful of stores. When they arrived at the biggest store in town, a discount retailer called Big-Mart, Nikki said, "I should be able to find something in here."

In the huge warehouse it took them almost ten minutes just to locate the shoes. She found a pair of simple white sneakers in her size, and headed to the girls' clothing section. She grabbed a pair of white-rimmed, light blue shorts that matched the light blue glove on her new t-shirt. They were her size, and so she made her way to the checkout with Spencer following behind her like a pet.

Back outside again, Spencer asked, "Where are you going to keep your stuff? You could just wear it under your regular clothes I guess."

"Nah, that will be too hot and bulky in the summer and besides, I can't wear my new sneakers around either. I'll just keep them in my treasure chest with the gloves. That way I can shrink them and have them in my pocket at all times."

"Excellent," Spencer said.

Spencer pulled out his list and crossed off the three items they had done so far, "Okay, we've helped the farmers, disposed of the fallen trees, and finished your superhero outfit. All that's left is for you to do something heroic and make sure that someone sees it."

Nikki was about to comment that there weren't many people she would be able to help in such a small town, when they heard someone yell, "Help! Please help!" At that very moment her bracelet let out a burst of light and she saw the image of the light blue gloves appear in the crystal.

Spencer said, "Great timing, Hamburger-Helper. Now's your chance to show what you can do! You go back in Big-Mart and change into your outfit, and I'll go see what the problem is." Before Nikki could respond, he was running off toward the sound.

Nikki's heart fluttered as she struggled to get changed in the small bathroom stall. Eventually she was ready; she was even able to tie her ponytail mask without Spencer's help. She was glad that no one had come into the bathroom while she was in there.

Once finished, she ran out of the store with her clothes in her hand and then snuck into an alley. Hiding behind a large dumpster, she opened the chest and swapped her clothes for the light blue gloves. Pressing her thumb to the bird symbol she said, "Here goes nothing," and without thinking too much about it, rocketed into the air, ready to meet her destiny.

20

Nikki saves Betsy

Spencer was easily able to locate the source of the distress call. At first he was a bit disappointed, but the more he thought about it, the more convinced he became that this would be the perfect opportunity for Nikki to be revealed to the people of Cragglyville. Using her flying gloves, it would be a simple task for her and she would be able to get the positive publicity they needed.

It was almost as if the cat was in on it and had climbed the tree just so it could be rescued by Nikki Powergloves. While not the most daring feat, in a small town where news was slow, it would get the full attention of the media. It must have been a particularly slow news day, because the local TV station crew had already arrived; they had probably been driving around town hoping that something would happen.

An old woman was crying under the tree. "Oh, my poor little Betsy, come down from that tree!"

Spencer approached her. "Is there something I can do, ma'am?"

"Oh, thank goodness you are here, young man. Are you a very good climber?" she asked expectantly.

"I'm afraid not. I am a little afraid of heights. If only there was a superhero nearby who could help."

The woman looked at him like he was nuts and reached up to her ear to turn up the volume on her hearing aid. "A superhero did you say? I think you've been reading too many comic books, young man."

"You never know," Spencer replied. The TV crew, which was comprised of a single camera man and a reporter, had their video equipment, a single camera and a microphone, out of the van and were looking up at the tree. "Hold on one second, ma'am, everything will be alright soon."

Spencer jogged over to the cameraman and said, "Hey, Spielberg, I think the best shot would be a wide angle that gets the entire sky as well as the cat in the tree. It will help to show just how high up the cat has managed to climb before getting stuck."

"What do you know, kid? I want to get a close-up of the cat's face to show just how scared it is," the man retorted.

"That's a bad idea," Spencer replied, before dashing back to the tree. Just as he looked up at the cat, he saw a flying shape appear on the horizon. It was moving so fast it was only a blur. Good girl, he thought, Nikki was giving the cameras plenty of time to capture her on film.

"Hey, mister," he yelled back to the cameraman. "What's that in the sky? It seems to be headed our way!"

The man pointed the camera toward the flying object and Spencer heard him say, "That's odd, I've never seen a bird like that."

The flying object came closer and closer—the camera moved with it across the sky—until it was almost on top of the tree. Spencer watched as Nikki, with a burst of speed, zipped deftly between the branches and grabbed the cat from its perch. She did one more flying lap around the tree and performed a perfect helicopter landing, with one arm holding the cat and the other on her hip, like you would expect from a confident superhero. She landed next to the old woman.

The old woman looked like she might faint, but managed to stammer, "Th-th-thank you. Who…Who are you?"

In a deep voice, Nikki said, "I'm Nikki Powergloves, and this town will never be in danger again with me around!" After handing the cat to the woman, she took off into the sky, her form becoming smaller and smaller until she disappeared from sight completely.

Spencer was grinning from ear to ear. *Way to go, Nikks!* he thought. Trying to remain calm, he remembered that he needed to pretend to be as surprised and amazed as the rest of the bystanders.

The reporter yelled to the cameraman, "Tell me you got that!"

"I got everything, sir."

"Good, let's roll with a live special report and you can add in the footage on my cue. Live in three…two…one…" The camera's light blinked red, alerting the reporter that the broadcast had begun.

The reporter declared, "This is Stephen Wallace at Channel Seven news, reporting from Main Street in Cragglyville. We have just witnessed a remarkable event. One that this town…no, that this *world* has never seen before. I'm sure that you all used to think that superheroes were something fictional from your childhood memories of comic books and cartoons, but I can definitively say that there is a real, live superhero in our town. She calls herself Nikki Powergloves and we just watched her miraculous recovery of a very frightened cat from the clutches of the uppermost branches of a tree."

Spencer liked this guy. He had a way of making even the easiest rescue sound more dangerous than wrestling a crocodile with both hands tied behind your back.

The reporter continued, "We take you now to the footage of the heroic rescue." After a few minutes of silence, while the TV station was likely broadcasting Nikki in action, Stephen Wallace went on to say, "There you have it, a brave act of pure selflessness, by what appeared to be a child superhero. We'll now interview a few of the witnesses."

First, he spoke to the old woman, who seemed to be in shock by the whole event. She kept stroking her cat while saying, "Thank you, Nikki, thank you" and, "I don't know how Betsy got away from me."

Next he turned to Spencer and to his surprise, Stephen's first question was, "Young man, do you have any idea who Nikki Powergloves really is?"

"I, uh, well…no, of course not. It was hard to see her and, well, I doubt she's even from around here," he managed to stammer out.

"So there's no chance she goes to your school?"

Spencer recovered quickly. "No chance at all, sir. Why would a superhero like that live in a town like this?"

Spencer's question stumped the reporter. "That's a very good question, son. One we may never know the answer to." He moved on to other bystanders that had witnessed the event and Spencer let out a sigh of relief. Time to go find Nikki.

21

Russian spies looking for Nikki?

Nikki saw Spencer pass the alleyway where she had just finished changing back into her regular clothes. She ran out behind him and yelled, "Hey, Spence!"

Spencer whirled around, his eyes widening in surprise. "But how did you..? I saw you fly out of sight, you must have been miles away."

Nikki grinned. "No distance is too far for my orange powergloves," she explained.

"Hmm, which ones were the orange ones...?" Spencer said to himself. Nikki started to open her mouth to speak, but Spencer interrupted. "Wait, don't tell me...not the animal ones, those were brown..." His eyes lit up as something clicked in his brain. "Ah, I remember, the ones with the shoes, the super-speed running gloves. Are you sure no one saw you though?"

"Positive. I can run so fast that it's like I'm just a blur. I even ran right past an old man on the street and he didn't even blink. Plus, I used a second powerglove to ensure no one could see me."

Spencer began to hum. He was probably trying to think about all the different gloves he had seen earlier that day. He said, "I give up, which other one did you use?"

"The invisibility one, of course. Now that I know I can combine powergloves, I will combine the invisibility gloves with the other ones whenever I don't want to be seen."

"That's brilliant, Albert-Einstein. You are already gaining the instincts of a true superhero."

"You really think so, Spence?"

"Absolutely."

They walked back to Nikki's house together, laughing and talking about how Nikki rescued the cat the whole way. When they arrived, Mrs. Nickerson—of course!—invited Spencer to dinner again, because his mom was working a double shift at the hospital. Dinner wouldn't be until seven, so when Mr. Nickerson arrived home from work, Nikki and Spencer sat on the couch with him to watch the six o'clock news.

The top story was about the miraculous rescue of a cat from a tree by a child superhero. Nikki's dad watched in amazement as they showed the footage of the four-and-a-half-foot masked girl swoop down from the sky and snatch the cat from high in the tree. The last ten seconds showed Nikki landing with the cat as she announced, "I'm Nikki Powergloves, and this town will never again be in danger with me around!" They were already comparing her to the masked girl who had flown down to scare the gorilla away from the Town Hall steps. The reporter believed they were the same girl.

Prepared for this moment, Nikki made her voice sound as natural as possible and said, "That's funny, she has the same first name as me." Her dad looked at her curiously. She continued, "Spencer saw the whole thing happen, didn't you, Spence?"

"I sure did, I think I may get on the news. Kazaaa!"

Mr. Nickerson's eyes widened as they cut to the interview with Spencer. He beamed proudly when it was over and said, "I was nervous, but I knew I needed to voice my opinion for the sake of the news."

Nikki's dad asked, "And where were you during all of this, Nikki?"

She was ready for this question as well. "I was using the bathroom at Big-Mart. I'm so angry I missed the coolest thing that has ever happened in this town." She impressed even herself as she managed a look of bitter disappointment on her face. Although he stared at her for a second, eventually her dad turned back to the news, seemingly convinced by her story. The next story came on and Mr. Nickerson's jaw dropped when he saw the full and healthy fields of corn that had popped up magically from the destroyed farmland. "But how...?" he murmured.

"That's amazing, huh, Nikks?" Spencer said, "I guess miracles still do happen."

"Yeah," Nikki said dumbly.

The news reporter was saying how there were rumors that Nikki Powergloves was responsible for the miracle plant growing, too. Without another word, Mr. Nickerson stood up and went into the kitchen to tell his wife about the news story.

Mrs. Nickerson didn't seem to fully believe her husband as he talked all through dinner about what they had seen on the news. "I just don't see how that's possible. It must be a trick of the cameras or a hoax or something," she said.

Spencer interjected, "Would I lie, Mrs. Nickerson? I know what I saw and it is exactly what was on the news."

"Of course I believe that you think you saw something miraculous, but I am just challenging whether there might be a more logical explanation for it. For example, when you watch a magician cut a woman in half with a saw, or make something disappear, do you think he really did it or that there is a trick to it?"

"Yeah, I see your point. Those are just illusions and there is always a trick that is hidden from the audience," he replied.

Mr. Nickerson said, "Yes, but this wasn't a stage somewhere, this was real life. And it was a young girl that did it, not some polished magician. I've been thinking about how, scientifically speaking, it could have been done, and I just can't come up with a logical answer. A rocket suit like Robert Downey Jr. used in *Iron Man* is totally out of the question, even the military hasn't been able to come up with anything feasible in that realm yet. She looked more like *Superman* to me. And re-growing crop fields in less than a day, it's impossible!"

Nikki had been quiet during the entire debate, because she was afraid to draw any attention to herself. Plus, it was fun to listen to her parents' theories when she knew the truth. Finally she spoke up: "What if the girl really does have powers?" Her parents stopped talking and looked at her. Spencer had a funny smirk on his face. "I'm just sayin', what if?"

Her mom said, "Well, that would be incredible and she could probably do a lot of good things for the world, but I'm sure there would be many scientists and government agencies that would want to talk to her about where she acquired her powers from."

Nikki's and Spencer's eyes locked. They had never talked about what consequences there might be to going public. What if the army came after her? Or the air force? Or worse yet, what if there were Russian spies out there looking for her right now? She was too young to become a test subject in some government lab somewhere. She lost her appetite.

Anxious to end the conversation, Nikki said, "I'm pretty full now, I think I may just turn in early tonight. It's been a long day. G'night, Spence."

"Bye, Nikks. I'll see you tomorrow."

22

The bomb

When Nikki woke up the next day, she was worried. All her jubilation from the previous day's rescue was gone and she was scared of being captured by the government, or Russian spies, or maybe even the mafia. Hoping to take her mind off of things, she logged onto her laptop.

The top local news headline was, "Nikki Powergloves Performs Astonishing Rescue." She read through the article. Most of it was as expected, with quotes from witnesses, a link to the video, and commentary on the event. She reached the last line, which read, "Nikki Powergloves and our town have become major National news and have captured the attention of people across the country." *Oh no*, she thought.

Switching to a National news website, Nikki found that her video had made the top-ten list for the day; she was currently sitting at number four. Needing to talk to the only other person that knew the truth, Nikki logged onto her instant messenger. As usual, Spencer was online. Their conversation went like this:

NikkNack14: hi spence

SpicNSpence29: hi N, u r big news, crikey!

NikkNack14: i saw, not happy

SpicNSpence29: don't worry

NikkNack14: how can i not worry? they will come 4 me soon

SpicNSpence29: u r 2 fast, they will never catch u. vroom vroom!

NikkNack14: thx, but still worried they will

SpicNSpence29: hang in there. we can lay low for now, come over later and we can play a game or something

NikkNack14: ok, be there soon

Nikki logged out and slammed the laptop lid shut. Tucking the laptop under her arm she rushed out of her room without doing any of her morning chores. She skipped breakfast and was barely able to answer her mom's question of "Where are you off to, Nikki?" with "Spencer's, be back soon," before she had run out the door.

When she arrived at Spencer's, he was eating a bowl of Chocolate Covered Sugar Wheats. He called it his brain food. Wheat was good for you, he reasoned. Nikki poured herself a bowl, too.

Between munch's, she said, "What am I going to do, Spence? I've been defeated by Jimmy twice now, destroyed half the town with my powers, and now there are all kinds of government people looking for me!"

Spencer tried to calm her down. "Look, Darkwing-Duck, I have never been involved in anything like this before, so I don't have all the answers. But what if you could ask anyone in the world, living or dead, what to do, who would you ask?"

Without hesitation she replied, "Grandpa Bernard."

"You knew your grandpa pretty well, Nikki. What do you think he would say to you?"

She hesitated. Closing her eyes, she tried to remember some of her favorite memories of her grandpa. Various images swirled through her mind, spinning and fading away. One image stuck with her and played clearly in her memory, like an old movie, in black and white. She was in a crowd of people lining a street. Children were laughing and running around. Some were eating ice cream or cotton candy. Somehow she was able to see everything clearly; it felt like she was above the crowd, levitating. Looking down, she noticed a familiar shiny head, ringed by wispy, gray hair. Grandpa Bernard! The details came whooshing back into her mind. She was sitting on his shoulders; it was the day of the 50th Annual Cragglyville 4th of July Parade, the year before her Grandpa died. When the mounted policemen passed by, she and Grandpa cheered especially loud. Next came the high school marching band and some other floats built by local business owners. Last was the Mayor's car, a shiny, black, classic Mercedes Benz convertible—"the finest car in the world," her grandpa called it. The mayor waved and honked his horn at the roaring crowds. Grandpa Bernard lifted Nikki high above his head and strode forward away from the townspeople and onto the road, on a collision course with the Mayor's car. The Mercedes stopped and he lifted her over the side, setting her down in the passenger's seat. Mayor Apple tousled her hair and said, "Welcome to the Parade, Nikki." She just smiled, in awe of the town leader. The crowd cheered louder. Later that day, Grandpa Bernard had said to her, "Today, Nikki, you were a star. But you will always be a star. My shining star. No matter what life throws at you, you will be able to handle it, because you are a star!"

"Nikki? Helloooo?"

Nikki shook her head and opened her eyes. Spencer was staring at her, waving a hand across her face. "I thought you fell asleep, zzzzzz," he said.

"No, I was just remembering something."

"About your grandpa?"

"Yes. He would have believed in me. He said I was a star."

"You are, Nikks. He was right."

119

"Thanks, Spence," she said, giving her friend a quick but warm hug. Her face was relaxed; there was no trace of the stress that had plagued her earlier.

At that moment, a blinding light burst from her powerbracelet and her face changed, a look of determination replacing her previously calm face.

"You're right, Spencer. As you said before, 'With great power comes great responsibility.' I can do this. Can I use your bathroom?"

Less than a minute later, she emerged as Nikki Powergloves, child superhero. Her hands were covered, one with a peach glove and the other with a gold glove. "Time to go," she said.

"Good luck, Ping-Pong-Ball," Spencer replied.

Nikki pressed the clock symbol on her gold glove and in a flash, the powerbracelet transported her to Main Street, outside of the bank. Unsure of what to do next, Nikki looked all around her, hoping to find a clue. She heard the door to the bank swing open and an old security guard with a bald head and a gray, curly mustache exited onto the sidewalk. Her bracelet pulsed in excitement; Nikki could feel the energy streaming through her bones.

Knowing by some instinct what she needed to do next, she followed the security guard halfway down the block, where he slipped into an alley and lit up a cigarette. Apparently, it was time for his break. Rather than follow him into the alley, Nikki pressed the identical stick figures symbol on her peach glove and rapidly transformed into the old security guard.

As she strode back down the sidewalk toward the bank, she couldn't help but to giggle when she saw her reflection in the shop windows that she passed. She looked so old...and so wrinkly!

Upon arriving at the bank, she entered quietly and tried to look like she belonged there. After all, she was the security guard and was probably allowed anywhere in the bank. She tried to close her mind off to all thoughts, except for why she had been brought to this place. As she allowed her instincts to guide her, she could feel the bracelet pulsing softly on her wrist.

Nikki strolled through the "Employees Only" gate, and a black man with glasses sitting at a teller's window, said, "Hey, Boggs, I thought you were going for a smoke."

Keeping her cool, Nikki replied in a voice that was foreign to her: the old man's voice. "Nah, tryin' to quit. That stuff will kill ya." She kept walking past the tellers and through a doorway that led into the bank offices. As she walked down the narrow hallway, the bracelet began to pulse faster. *I must be heading in the right direction*, she thought.

The hall ended in a "T" and she let her instincts turn her to the right, which led her to a door with a sign on it that read, "Restricted Access to Authorized Personnel Only." Now she was getting somewhere.

She noticed that when she took on the appearance of the old man, she obtained not only his clothes, but everything that was in his pockets, including his keys and ID card. She swiped the ID against a small electronic reader on the wall, and the door made a clicking sound. Pushing the door open slowly, she peeked into the area beyond. It was the bank vault!

The massive steel vault door appeared to be more secure than Fort Knox and for a second, she wondered why she could possibly have been brought here. If someone was going to try to rob the bank, they would need a small army to get through the door. But the bracelet was pulsing wildly now, so she knew she was in the right place. There was nowhere else to go but into the vault. But how would she get in?

She sat down behind a large water pipe in the corner to think, hoping that the answer might present itself. Just in the nick of time, she pulled her knees to her chest, obscuring her entire body from view. She heard the closed door open again, and a short man wearing spectacles and carrying a cane entered the room. Nikki poked one eye out from behind the pipe and watched the man.

He was mumbling something, most of which Nikki couldn't hear, but she was able to pick up a few words. "Darn Mrs Peppers….she always…got to get her diamonds…" Nikki heard a series of beeps as the man entered the code for the vault. The steel door groaned open. Just as Nikki was considering leaving her hiding spot to follow him into the vault, the man gasped.

"Oh my gosh. A bomb? But how? Ten seconds?" He rushed out of the vault and through the door into the hallway, not bothering to close the vault door. The words, "*a bomb…ten seconds*," rang through Nikki's head. How could she diffuse a bomb in only ten seconds?

23

Nikki blows up a lake

She sprang into action, rushing from her hiding place like a bomb was about to go off. Oh wait, a bomb *was* about to go off! Leaping into the vault, Nikki discovered a large nest of explosives at the back of the chamber.

Blue digital numbers counted down the timer. Seven, six, five…Nikki's mind was racing. She felt like she was missing something. There wasn't time to diffuse it and she wouldn't know how to anyway. She could close the vault door and seal the bomb inside, but the money would still be destroyed. Four, three, two…What was she missing?

It hit her like a ton of bricks. The timer changed to one second as she pushed her thumb to the clock symbol on her gold glove and shut her eyes. Every cell of her brain was focused on one thing: *Stop time*.

She heard a strange rumbling sound. Her life flashed before her eyes as Nikki knew she was too late—the bomb was exploding. She waited to go to heaven or hell or wherever she was destined for, but then one second slowly passed. And another second. If the bomb *did* go off, wouldn't she be dead already?

Nikki opened her eyes. Everything in the vault looked the same, except for the bomb, which had broken apart and was levitating in four large pieces, along with numerous fragments of shrapnel. A mix of fire and smoke hung in the air like a foggy sunrise. The scene looked like she had been watching an action movie and pressed pause on her remote control just after an explosion.

Nikki wondered what to do next. It was obvious that if she started time again, the bomb would continue to explode and blow the money, the bank, and her to smithereens. She had to find a way to get the bomb pieces outside and away from everyone and everything.

Her first instinct was to switch her gloves to two powers that would help her, but she realized that she needed to be very careful and remember not to remove the gold glove, because it was the only thing keeping time stopped and preventing her from dying a very quick and explosive death.

She peeled off the peach glove while holding her breath, unsure as to whether removing one glove would interfere with the power of the other one. Time remained frozen and she let out a big sigh of relief. The only change was that her body transformed from the old security guard back into Nikki Powergloves, complete with her superhero costume and hair-mask.

As she reopened the treasure chest, she considered the benefits of each of the various powergloves she could choose. First, she needed to contain the fragments of the explosion. *A heavy dose of ice should do the trick*, she thought, grabbing one of the white gloves.

Soon she had coated the explosion with a thick layer of ice, which made it look like some crazy piece of art you would find at an ice sculpting exhibit. Given the size of the bomb and the weight of the ice, the next decision was easy. She would need her super-strength.

In seconds, she had swapped the white glove for a purple one, and had hoisted the icy explosion onto one shoulder. She retraced her steps through the vault door, the secondary door, and into the hallway. Halfway down the hall she passed the short man, who had been in full stride when the clock had stopped ticking. Heading back into the public portion of the bank, she saw people lined up at the teller windows, going about their business, without any knowledge that they had nearly been blown up. For now, they would have to remain stuck in time.

She lugged the ice outside and carried it down Main Street, as if she were a pizza delivery boy making a regular delivery. Despite the urgency of the situation, she couldn't help but laugh as she passed various scenes, now frozen in time. On her right, a dog's leg was lifted and a yellowish stream shot from his undercarriage onto a tree. On her left, a little boy had a finger jammed up his nose, while his mom's finger scolded him for digging for gold in public.

Within 15 minutes, Nikki had reached the outer limits of the commercial district and was into rural Cragglyville. As she walked, she looked for a place to safely explode the bomb. Ideally, she would fly it into outer space and blow it up there, but she couldn't use her super-strength and her flying ability while still using the gold glove to stop time.

Based on some of the movies she had seen, another good option would be to get the bomb underwater, so she kept her eyes peeled for any farm lakes. Eventually, she found one that couldn't be any more perfect—it was a large pond that was set more than a hundred yards away from the main farmhouse. She carried the bomb to the lake and jumped into the water with it still on her shoulder. The ice floated and she kicked her legs to propel herself forwards, like a swimmer with a paddle board.

When she reached the approximate center of the pond, she left the ice to melt and swam back to shore. Nikki waited patiently for the bomb to submerge. Once she was sure it had sunk to the bottom, she removed her gold glove.

KABOOM!! The sound was deafening, as a mountain of water erupted from the lake. It was like the fattest man in the world had just done a cannonball off of the high dive at the swimming pool. Nikki was sprayed by a thousand droplets of water that were carried on the wind, but she didn't care because she was already wet. She had saved the day and this time it was more than just a cat from a tree. Real human lives had been saved.

She knew what Spencer would want her to do: make an appearance. Nikki returned the gold glove to the chest and switched it for the light blue one. *There is something about flying that catches people's attention*, she thought. Just as she took off into the air, she saw a farmer run out of the house waving his fist at her. *Sorry, Mister*, she thought, *you can't please everyone all the time.*

She zoomed back to town, where there was already a commotion outside the bank. The short man, who it turns out was the bank manager, was explaining to the police what had happened. He was clearly very confused by the fact that, in his eyes, the bomb had mysteriously disappeared shortly after he had seen its timer counting down to zero.

One of the people saw Nikki coming and shouted, "Look! It's Nikki Powergloves!" The crowds' eyes shifted to where the woman was pointing, and they started to cheer as she swooped in. With her adrenaline pumping, Nikki landed on top of the bank, not wanting to be too close to the camera crews, who had just arrived on the scene.

She stood, looking down at the people, not knowing what she should say. A woman reporter took control. "What happened here today, Nikki?"

Nikki deepened her voice and said, "There is no reason to panic. There was a bomb in the bank vault, but I disposed of it." Upon hearing the word "bomb", a frightened hush fell over the crowd.

Someone yelled, "Thank you, Nikki!"

Nikki was about to bow to the crowd and fly off, when the woman reporter fired off another question. "Nikki, how is it that you seem to always be in the right place at the right time? How do we know that you didn't plant the bomb and then remove it, so you could save the day and look like a hero?"

Nikki was stunned by the question. How could this woman suggest that she was a villain when Nikki had just saved a whole bunch of people? "Because I wouldn't do that," she said, her voice taking on an irritated edge to it.

"Then who did plant the bomb?"

"I have no idea, but I will not rest until the villain is brought to justice!" Nikki declared. Not wanting to deal with any more questions from the nosy reporter, Nikki decided this was a good time to make her exit. For effect, she did a swan dive off the roof and swooped down over the heads of the crowd, before rocketing into the sky.

24

From hero to zero

Nikki landed behind the tool shed in her backyard and changed out of her Nikki Powergloves outfit. She went straight to Spencer's place. He apparently hadn't left the house while she was gone, which was not that surprising considering she had only been gone for an hour.

"An hour?" Nikki questioned. "It feels like I've been gone all day. Being a superhero is hard work."

"I saw you on the news—it was live. Wowsers!" Spencer said.

"And? How'd I do?"

"You were great, Nikki, especially when you were dealing with that annoying Susan Hughes from the Crag. What a dunce!" The Cragglyville Daily, or "the Crag", as everyone called it, was the local newspaper.

"Do you think she will print anything bad about me?"

"I don't see how she could. You saved the day. Cha-ching!"

"I don't know, Spencer. It seems like she's out to get me."

"I wouldn't worry about her. We have more important things to deal with."

"Like what? Washing my outfit? It kind of smells like stale pond water." Nikki went on to tell Spencer the rest of the story and how she had cleverly disposed of the bomb in the lake.

"That was brilliant, Nikks! But now it's my turn. You got another e-mail from Jimmy while you were gone." He flipped open Nikki's laptop and read:

"Dear NP,

I love your new name! Who came up with that, you or Spencer? I would guess it was Spencer, he seems to be the brains of the operation. Now listen here, if you won't meet me, then you will have to keep saving people around town. The bomb that you so miraculously handled today was planted by me. You are probably asking yourself, how could a nine-year-old boy like me install a sophisticated explosive device in a fortified steel vault in a bank? Let's just say, I have powers too, Nikki. So, whaddya say, should we meet, or should I continue to terrorize your precious town of Cragglyville?

Yours truly,

JP"

The anger boiled up inside of Nikki's stomach and erupted into her head. There was practically steam coming out of her ears. "Give me the computer, Spencer," she ordered.

"Now wait just one second, Nikks, we need to think about this logically before we do anything rash. I know you are angry, but we need to be smart about this or things could get really bad."

Nikki took a few deep breaths and was gradually able to relax. "Okay, I'm calm. Let's talk about it. My first question is: why did he sign his name 'JP'? Up until now he has called himself Jimmy, and his calling card in San Francisco said 'Jimmy- Boy Wonder'. Maybe he's giving us a clue as to his last name by showing his initials."

"I doubt it. Clearly the 'J' is for Jimmy, but wait a minute, I wonder..." he trailed off.

"What, Spence?"

"Well, in his latest e-mail he addressed you as 'NP' for 'Nikki Powergloves', and now he signs his name as 'JP', which I would expect means 'Jimmy Power…something'. He said he has seen a Weeble just like you have, and he mentions in his e-mail that he has powers, too. Maybe he has powergloves just like you!"

"But you think he just chooses to use his powers for evil?"

"Possibly. And his powers may be completely different than yours. He seems to be able to do things that might be harder for you, like planting a bomb in a vault. But maybe he doesn't have a lot of the powers that you have, like super-strength and super-speed."

Nikki had heard enough, she was ready to respond. She typed:

"Hi Jimmy Power_____,
Bring it on.
NP"

They waited for Jimmy's response, but it never came. Eventually they became bored and spent the afternoon watching the news. At first, most of the coverage was pretty positive, with the reporters talking about how Nikki had saved the day. The bank manager was interviewed and he poured out numerous compliments about what a fine young citizen Nikki Powergloves was, and how he wished there were more like her in Cragglyville. Nikki's cheeks went red at all of the attention, but was happy to hear it. She felt like a true hero.

It wasn't until Stephen Wallace showed up at the site of the explosion that things started to go badly. He began by interviewing the angry farmer. "This is Stephen Wallace with Channel 7 News. I have with me Mr. Cameron, who owns a farm about a mile from town. Would you tell me what happened here, sir?"

The camera zoomed in on a gruff-looking man with a massive beard. He was wearing blue overalls and big black boots. He was covered from head to foot with dirt. "I'll tell yer exactly what happen'd 'ere. I's mindin' my own business, tryin' to take a break from a mornin' of back breakin' work, when I see, off yonder by the pond, a little pipsqueak of a girl, luggin' a big ol' block of ice into my pond. I watched 'er out my window as she jumped in my pond, swam that there ice into the middle of my lake and sunk it. She swam back to shore and I was about to go back to my relaxin' when I hear an explosion like yer ain't never heard in your life, I can promise yer that. It all happened real quick, like someone had pressed fast forward on the remote. An' I couldn't move while she was doin' it, like I was frozen.

"I ran out to try 'n catch 'er, but she flew off like a dang bird. It was the darndest thing I ever saw."

Stephen Wallace nodded. "And how do you feel now, sir?"

"I'm angry, of course I am. Look at what she's done to my poor fish," he waved his hand across the width of the pond in the background. The cameraman panned across the lake. Dozens of dead fish had risen to the surface and now floated up and down, like apples bobbing in a barrel at some Halloween party.

"But don't you think the girl deserves some credit? She did save a lot of lives today," Wallace challenged.

"Sure she does," the farmer answered, "but she also needs to take responsibility for 'er actions. I'm sure there are plenty of other places she could have taken that there bomb, rather than my pond."

Before Wallace could ask another question, there was a screeching sound and a fog of dust clouded the scene. The camera turned and zoomed in on a green van that had pulled into the drive and parked next to the TV equipment. Through the dusty haze, the picture showed that stenciled on the side of the van in blue lettering was, "Environmental Protection Council".

Out jumped three people: two men and one woman. They strode over to where the interview was being conducted and flanked Stephen Wallace. The farmer looked embarrassed and slunk out of the picture, as far away from the camera as he could get.

Wallace looked surprised by the intrusion, but he recovered by asking, "What brings the EPC to Cragglyville?"

A man with a dark mustache, who was wearing a cowboy's hat, answered, "We heard about the environmental disaster here at this poor farm, and we felt we needed to act. Dark is the day when an attack on the environment, like the one we had today, goes unpunished."

Wallace sounded like a parrot as he repeated the same question he had posed to the farmer just a few minutes earlier. "But don't you think the girl deserves some credit? Her quick actions saved lives today."

A woman with a long braid, a long nose, and a long chin responded by saying, "Yes, of course, she saved some lives, but that doesn't mean she shouldn't be held accountable for the way in which she saved those lives. She had a complete disregard for the environment and for that, she will face the full resources of the Environmental Protection Council."

The TV turned off and Nikki turned to see Spencer holding the remote control. "Hey! I was watching that!" she said.

"Well, I say we are done watching that nonsense. These people are unbelievable! You save all those people from a quick and explosive death, and they try to treat you like a common criminal! I won't stand for it, Nikki. I'm going to march right down to Town Hall and demand that a parade be held in your honor! Holy cow!"

Nikki waited until Spencer had finished his tirade before saying, "Thanks, Spence. I really do appreciate the thought, but it's really not necessary. They're probably right, I should have thought about what I was doing before blowing up a bomb in some poor farmer's lake. This is our home town and we need to treat it with respect. After all, we have so many happy memories here. Tomorrow, Nikki Powergloves will make a public appearance. I will see what I can do to help clean up the mess, and hopefully the environmental people will drop the charges."

"But you did nothing wrong! It's not fair, Nikks."

"Maybe so, but it's the right thing to do, Spence. If I want the people to like me and think of me as a true superhero, I have to listen to their concerns."

Spencer didn't look convinced, but he said, "Okay, you're the Big-Boss-Man."

Trying to change the subject, Nikki said, "Let's check to see if Jimmy has responded yet."

Spencer opened the laptop and located Nikki's e-mail program. Handing it to her, he said, "You do it."

She clicked the button for "Send/Receive" and a new message popped up.

"NP,

How are you feeling? I've been watching the news and people around there don't seem to like you too much. This is the way it always starts and trust me, I have a lot more experience than you in this area. You'll try so hard to get them to like you, but guess what? They never will. Every good thing you do will be thrown back in your face. They will treat you like a villain, instead of the hero you really are. We are a lot alike, Nikki, you just don't see it yet. But since you asked me to 'bring it on', I will. Hopefully after this next one, you will agree to meet me, and you will understand why I do what I do. Good luck.

JP

P.S. Wouldn't it be a shame if something happened over at Farmer Miller's place?"

After reading the last line of the message, Nikki jumped up. "I gotta go, Spence. Farmer Miller is in trouble!"

"Wait a minute, can't you just stay here until the powerbracelet lights up? Jimmy might not even do anything today."

"The bracelet is useful, but it doesn't tell me until after something has already happened, like a cat getting stuck in a tree or a bomb being planted in a vault. I want to be there before he does anything so I can stop him completely, rather than just trying to clean up the mess afterwards."

Spencer knew she was right, so he gave up the argument and instead, gave his friend a hug and said, "Be careful, Nikki, this kid is very dangerous."

She hugged him back and said, "Don't worry, I'll be fine. I'll come back as soon as it is over." She went into the other room and moments later emerged as Nikki Powergloves—she was ready for action. In her hands were two gloves: one light blue and one gray. Slipping on the flying glove, she said, "I'll start with flying and invisibility, and hopefully I can surprise him. Later I can switch to whichever gloves I need to stop him."

She put on the gray glove and, instantly, her body was gone, but her voice was still there. "Bye, Spencer," she said. He followed her footsteps to the back door and watched as it opened, seemingly on its own. Before closing the door, Spencer yelled, "I'll picture you rocketing into the sky—Nikki Powergloves to the rescue!"

25

Getting hit in the head by a lightning bolt hurts

As she flew toward the Miller's, Nikki thought about what Jimmy might be planning. He could burn their house down, or plant another bomb. Destroying their crops was another option, but she was less worried about that, since she had the ability to regrow them. She thought back to the last time she had seen the Millers. They had been so welcoming, sharing fresh warm apple pie and cider. She had to save them. The scariest of the possibilities was that he might do something to hurt one of them. She tried not to think about it. Whatever he tried, she was going to stop him.

When she arrived at the farm, she circled the perimeter four or five times before feeling comfortable that Jimmy wasn't there yet. Being invisible had its perks: she didn't have to worry about being spotted while she conducted her surveillance. She landed without a sound on the roof of the main house, from where she felt she would best be able to watch the entire farm. Every few minutes, she would scan a different direction to ensure she saw him coming from a long way off. First north…then south…east…west. Repeat.

There is no way he will be able to sneak up on me, Nikki thought, as she looked toward the back of the house. Just then, a boy materialized out of thin air about halfway across the backyard. One moment the yard was empty, and the next he was there.

He was wearing a black costume, complete with a gray belt, black mask, and black cape. On his chest were two letters that Nikki wasn't quite able to see, but knew what they were: JP. It was him.

However, out of everything he was wearing, his mismatched boots stood out the most. On one foot he was wearing a brown boot and on the other he had on a bright yellow boot that looked like the galoshes that Nikki sometimes wore in the rain. Nikki thought about how she was currently wearing a different colored glove on each hand. *It is too similar to be just a coincidence*, she thought. His powers came from his boots! JP stood for Jimmy Power*boots*!

She watched him, ready to spring into action at the slightest sign of trouble. Instead, Jimmy crouched low to the ground and remained completely still. Nikki stretched one of her legs to try to get more comfortable while she waited. As she repositioned herself, her foot gently scraped the roof, making a soft scratching noise.

Jimmy's ears perked up, his head popped up, and he stared directly at the spot where she was sitting. *Has my invisibility stopped working?* she wondered. She looked at her arm, but even she couldn't see it. Feeling uncomfortable under the piercing eyes of Jimmy's stare, Nikki remained frozen. After several minutes, he looked away from her and leaned down again, like an animal listening for any signs of danger. That was when Nikki realized that one of the boots he was wearing must give him super-hearing ability.

She decided to test her theory by, ever so slightly, scraping her toe on the roof again. The sound that she made was barely even loud enough for her to hear, but sure enough, Jimmy's head jolted up and his eyes locked in on her exact position. Again, after a few minutes,

Jimmy returned to all fours. After waiting patiently for ten minutes or so, he finally seemed satisfied that he wasn't in any danger and stood up.

To Nikki's surprise, he reached in his pocket and dug out a tiny object, which he set down on the ground. After taking a few steps back, he gave an invisible string a familiar tug, like Nikki had done so many times before, and the tiny object grew into a large treasure chest. Jimmy removed both of his boots and tossed them in the box. He reached inside the chest and extracted two different boots—one was fire-engine red and the other neon orange—and promptly put them on. Nikki wondered what terrible powers those boots would give him.

She figured she was about to find out as Jimmy raised his arm. He pointed his index finger directly toward the farmhouse, like a sniper aiming at his target. Nikki leapt off the roof and shot toward Jimmy, colliding with him seconds later. He tumbled backwards for several yards, coming to a stop after four or five somersaults.

Nikki winced, pain shooting through her shoulder from the impact. Jimmy recovered and jumped to his feet, flames bursting from the soles of his boots. The eruption of fire propelled him away from the ground. Ignoring the pain, Nikki gave chase.

It became a game of aerial follow-the-leader, as Jimmy did everything he could to throw her off his trail. Even though he couldn't see her, some sixth sense seemed to be telling him where Nikki was, as he rolled and ducked, changing directions every couple of seconds. Easily able to match his speed, Nikki stayed with him despite all of his efforts.

As she followed him, Nikki wondered what powers the second boot gave him. One boot allowed him to rocket through the air like a missile, but what was he trying to do when he pointed his finger at the house?

As she was thinking this, Jimmy dove sharply toward the ground, skimming along the surrounding fields. She saw him stretch his arm to the side and point a single finger at a bale of hay when they passed it.

He whipped his arm backwards and behind him, in the general direction that Nikki was chasing him from. In a flash, the hay bale shot through the air and collided with the side of Nikki's head, knocking her off of her trajectory.

She fell toward the earth, but managed to catch herself in mid-fall and land in a half run, like a seasoned sky-diver. Spitting out pieces of straw from her mouth, she looked up to see where Jimmy was. He had stopped in midflight and was looking directly at her. *But how can he see me?* she wondered. Looking down at where her arm should be, Nikki saw that there were clumps of hay floating in the air. In reality, the hay was stuck to her, but because she was invisible, all that Jimmy could see was the hay-outline of Nikki.

Knowing that she needed to switch her invisibility glove for another one that would be more useful, she opened her own treasure chest on the lawn. Throwing her gray glove inside, she rummaged through the remaining gloves, frantically trying to decide which one to use. "Which one, which one, which one?" she mumbled to herself. Before she had a chance to decide, she heard a sharp cracking sound behind her.

She whirled around to see the house shaking, as if a supernatural force was trying to pluck it from its moorings. A large crack appeared at the base of the house and the ground was rumbling from the tension. It felt like the house was built on a fault line, and the plates had shifted, causing an earthquake under her feet. Jimmy was levitating above the house like a god on Mount Olympus, his finger pointed at the roof. He was straining under the pressure, his body shaking, but ever so slowly, the house was obeying his command and rising from its foundation.

Her bracelet pulsed with light and Nikki looked into the crystal. It displayed both a purple glove and a black-and-yellow glove. It was time for super-strength and thunder and lightning! She located the required gloves and put them on.

The house had now pulled completely from the ground and was rising into the sky. Splinters of wood and cracked stone crumbled from its base as it rose. Water burst from broken pipes and electricity crackled along severed wires. But none of that mattered now. She had to stop him before the house rose too high.

Nikki sprinted for the floating house and just before reaching it, saw the front door open, and a terrified Mrs. Miller look out in horror. When Nikki reached the house, it was already ten feet in the air, which was well out of her normal jumping range, but with her leg muscles bulging with super-strength, she planted her left foot and pushed off with her right, leaping high into the air.

She grabbed onto the first of three steps that rose to the doorway, and using every ounce of her super-strength, pulled downwards with a powerful thrust. The house shuddered under the strain as Nikki tried to counteract the force that was pulling it in the opposite direction. Tiny cracks began to form on the outer walls and, for a second, Nikki thought that she and Jimmy might tear the house into two pieces.

With a mournful groan, the house slowly began to descend back toward the earth. Nikki wasn't sure whether she was winning the battle until she felt her dangling feet touch the ground. With all her might, she dug her feet into the dirt and drove the house downwards. The house smashed into its original location with a thundering crash, the impact sending vibrations through the earth.

Afraid that Jimmy might try to raise it again, Nikki pressed the lightning bolt symbol on her black-and-yellow glove and imagined a concentrated storm forming over the spot where a very surprised Jimmy Powerboots was still hovering. A black cloud appeared over him. A bolt of lightning seared through the air, connecting with Jimmy's skull and showering him with sparks.

His lifeless body dropped from the sky, as gravity regained its hold on him. Instinctively, Nikki ran the ten or so steps that she needed, and caught him before he could plow into the earth. Mrs. Miller stumbled out of the damaged, but intact house, and fell to her knees in gratitude. As sirens sounded in the distance, Nikki knew that the farmer's wife must have called 9-1-1 when the house first started to lift off. That was Nikki's cue to exit.

Still holding Jimmy in one arm, she replaced the lids on each treasure chest and pocketed them. Nikki ran as fast and as far away as she could, until she was well out of sight of the farmhouse. Taking a moment to catch her breath, she lowered Jimmy to the ground and pulled his boots off—his face was pale and he looked like he might be dead. She needed to get help fast, so she replaced her weather-controlling glove with her flying one, scooped him up, and launched herself into the sky.

26

How to save a villain

When she was halfway home, it all became too much for her. The adrenaline from the battle had worn off, and her mind replayed the entire brutal experience in a series of snapshots. The look of terror in Mrs. Miller's eyes; the crumbling and tearing house; the malicious look on Jimmy's face as he performed his evil acts; and finally, the harsh realization that she might have used her powers to kill another human being, and a kid at that. The image of Jimmy's pale face tore through her mind.

Her face was wet; tears were streaming down her cheeks. Her breathing became irregular while she choked out sobs. She tasted the salty liquid on her lips.

She landed in Spencer's backyard in plain view, without regard for caution. Bursting through the back door, she stood in the kitchen, trying to catch her breath. Hearing the door open, Spencer ran from the living room. When he saw her holding Jimmy's crumpled body, he asked, "What happened, Nikki?"

"I think I might have killed him!" she cried. Spencer grabbed him from her and gently set him on the tile floor. Nikki collapsed in a heap next to him.

"How did it happen?"

"I hit him with a bolt of lightning. I swear, I had no other choice, Spence."

"Don't worry about that now. Go and find me some towels and wet them with warm water."

Obediently, Nikki ran upstairs to the linen closet and found two hand towels. Using the bathtub, she soaked them in warm water and rung them out. She raced back downstairs and handed them to Spencer. She watched as her friend checked Jimmy's vital signs. First, he placed two fingers on Jimmy's neck, feeling for a pulse.

"He's got a pulse, but it's weak," Spencer said. Jimmy's stomach was rising and falling regularly—his breathing appeared to be normal.

Spencer placed one of the warm towels on Jimmy's forehead and another on his stomach. "What are you doing?" Nikki asked.

"I don't know," Spencer admitted. "But it just feels like the right thing to do."

Nikki nodded.

Spencer noticed that Jimmy's feet were bare. "Where are his shoes?" he asked.

Nikki's face was stained with tears, but she was feeling better and answered firmly, "He was wearing boots. I took them from him. They are the source of his power."

"Jimmy Power*boots*?" Spencer asked.

"That's right," Nikki replied.

"He spent a lot more time on his costume than you did," Spencer joked, trying to lighten the mood.

Nikki didn't even crack a smile. "Is he going to be alright?" she asked.

"I think so. He's breathing and he has a pulse, so I think he'll be fine. He probably just needs to sleep it off."

At that moment, Jimmy let out a heavy sigh and then groaned. Trying to sit up, he said, "Hey, let go of me," when Spencer held him down.

"It's not a good idea, Jimmy. You need to rest."

He raised his head to look down at his feet. "Gimme my powerboots back, Nikki," he demanded.

"Forget about it, Jimmy. You are never getting them back."

"You don't understand anything, Nikki. We are two of a kind and should be helping each other, not fighting each other."

"I think that sounds like a great idea. Why don't you help me try to do some good in this world?"

"Not a chance. I've tried that and it doesn't work. Every time I tried to help someone, it backfired on me. I remember this one time that I helped catch a couple of shoplifters. They were running down the street with a bunch of stolen stuff, and I hit them with a perfectly timed powerstomp—"

"What's a powerstomp?" Spencer interrupted.

"Don't worry about it, smarty-pants, it's just one of my powers. Anyway, the powerstomp tripped them up and they dropped all of the stolen stuff. I held them down until the police could arrive and then, guess what? The little punks accused me of assaulting them, and the police *believed* them, can you believe that? They said they would have to notify my parents and that I would probably end up goin' to juvie. I was not about to do that, so I used my powers to escape and I've been on the run ever since. When I found out about you, Nikki, I knew we were the same. I thought we could be partners, like Bonnie and Clyde—famous outlaws. Whaddya say?"

"I say that you're out of your mind! I will never be partners with you, and you are never getting your powerboots back. In fact, if I ever see your face around here again, I will not be nearly as nice as I was this time."

"What? This isn't the way it was supposed to happen," Jimmy said, confusion crossing his face.

Nikki had had enough of Jimmy Powerboots for one day. She grabbed him, and amidst his protests, ran out the door into the backyard, and shot upwards into the sky.

27

Villains never give up

The next two weeks of summer passed by quickly, as they fell into a routine. Nikki and Spencer spent nearly every day together, but never tired of each other's company. They played video games, hung out in the The Clubhouse, and went swimming at the pool. From time to time, Nikki's bracelet would pulse, and she would rush off to perform her duties as a superhero.

The issue with the bomb in the pond had eventually blown over—the tree-huggers had dropped all charges. The people in the town had not been too happy when the Environmental Protection Council seemed to place more value on a couple of fish than on real human lives. Cragglyville really came through for Nikki. Now they cheered for her whenever she swooped in. She had returned the statue of Arthur Munroe on his horse, and a project was underway to repair and restore the monument.

Even the news was mostly positive, calling her "a true superhero" and "the best thing that has ever happened to this town." Occasionally, Susan Hughes, the nasty newspaper writer, would write a scathing article in The Crag about how Nikki Powergloves was a menace to society and should be run out of town, but it didn't bother Nikki too much as no one seemed to agree with Susan.

Now, Nikki and Spencer were sitting on a couple of swings in the park talking about her latest superhero act—she had pulled four-year-old twin sisters out of a burning apartment—when her cell phone rang. She answered, "Hello?"

"Hello, Nikki Powergloves. Congratulations, it seems like you've been busy since we last met. I've been following the news very closely."

She immediately recognized the voice and replied, "Ahh, Jimmy Not-so-powerboots. How has life been treating you since you lost all of your powers?"

"Very, very good actually. You see, I've discovered something that I thought you might be interested in."

"And what might that be?" she asked.

"I've learned that the treasure chests we found are not unique."

"What do you mean?" Nikki asked.

"I mean that there are more kids just like us, who met Weebles, found treasure chests, and now have powers that they only dreamed of having. In fact, I made a new friend that I thought you might want to talk to. He understands me like no one ever has before. We've become partners."

Before she could reply a new voice came on the line. "Hi, Nikki, my name is Peter Powerhats. One of *my* powers is that I can find the exact location of any powerchest in the world, no matter how well it is hidden. I've recently been doing some work for Jimmy here."

Jimmy's voice came back on the line. "That's right, Nikki. With Peter's help I've finally been able to get back what was rightfully mine: my powerboots. And guess what? Now we are coming for you, Nikki. Good luck." The call went dead before Nikki could say anything in return.

"That's not possible," Nikki said, almost to herself.

Spencer had only heard bits and pieces of the conversation so he asked, "What's not possible, Nikks?"

She looked at him with concern etched across her forehead. "Jimmy said he has a friend who has powers and who helped him recover his lost treasure chest."

"Another kid with powers?" Spencer asked.

"Yep, he says there are lots of kids with powers. His friend, Peter Powerhats, can find lost treasure chests. Jimmy says they already found his. I don't know whether to believe him though, he may just be tricking me."

"We better check now, Nikks."

Nikki nodded, and the pair ran off toward Nikki's house. When they reached her yard, they cut along the side between the houses, and through the gate into the backyard. Nikki cautiously opened the door to her dad's tool shed. Earlier that summer when Nikki had defeated Jimmy, she and Spencer spent an afternoon prying up a couple of floorboards in the shed, digging a small hole, and, after hiding Jimmy's miniature treasure chest, nailing the floorboards back down.

"He wasn't lying," Nikki said when they entered the shed. Two floorboards had been pulled up, and the hole was empty. Jimmy had recovered his powerboots and he was coming back to Cragglyville.

"Are you worried?" Spencer asked.

Nikki looked defiant. "No, I beat him once and I can do it again," she said with determination in her voice.

Spencer didn't look convinced. "Yeah, but the last time it wasn't two against one. You know that he's going to bring this Peter Powerhats character with him this time. You won't stand a chance if you are outnumbered."

"We'll see about that," Nikki said. At that very moment, her phone vibrated as she received a text message. "If that is another threat from Jimmy, I might just go and find him instead of waiting for him to turn up here." They huddled around her phone to see what the message said.

u r not alone NP
there r other kids like u
most r not like JP and PP
we will come 2 help

Nikki and Spencer looked at each other, their eyes opening wide with wonder.

"This is awesome," Spencer said.

Nikki nodded and sent a reply:

thx, that is good 2 hear
who r u?

Her phone buzzed again when the reply came seconds later:

Samantha Powerbelts
c u soon

Upon reading the message, Nikki snapped her phone shut and dashed out of the shed. Spencer yelled, "Wait, Nikki! Where are you going?" and raced after her.

Nikki had hidden behind a bush and when Spencer exited the shed, she grabbed him from behind. With a *whoosh!* they were airborne. On many occasions, Spencer had asked Nikki if she would take him flying with her. But she always turned him down; she didn't think her powers were meant to be used for joyriding. For some reason, when she found out that there were other good kids with powers like hers, she changed her mind and decided to take Spencer on the wildest thrill ride of his life. For almost an hour she twisted and turned and ducked and dived around town.

Finally, as dusk approached, she found the tallest tree in town and landed like a bird, in its uppermost branches. She set Spencer on a wide branch and sat down next to him. As the sun splashed onto the horizon in a myriad of colors, Nikki put her arm around him and said, "No matter what happens, you will always be my best friend, Spence."

Spencer replied, "Thanks, Marshmallow-Man. And no matter what happens, you will always be the greatest superhero this world has ever known. I would say you can officially be called Nikki Powergloves. Cowabunga!"

Nikki grinned at her friend.

They both became lost in their imaginations, as they daydreamed about what wonderful adventures tomorrow would bring.

THE END (of this Adventure!)

Keep reading for a peek into David Estes's exciting Nikki Powergloves sequel, *Nikki Powergloves and the Power Council*.

Hero Card

Hidden Identity: Nikki Powergloves
Birth Name: Nikki Nickerson
Age: 9
Height: 4 feet, 2 inches
Weight: 67 pounds
Sidekick: Spencer Quick, certified genius
Known Allies: Samantha Powerbelts
Source of Power: Gloves

Powers

Glove Color	Glove Picture	Power
White	Snowflake	Create ice
Red	Flame	Create fire
Light blue	Bird	Fly
Black & yellow	Lightning Bolt	Control the weather
Green	Leaf	Super-grow plants
Purple	Muscly arm	Super-strength
Orange	Shoes	Super-speed
Gray	No picture	Invisibility
Brown	Paw print	Transform into an animal
Pink	Tarot card	See the future
Gold	Clock	Freeze or slow down time
Peach	Two identical stick figures	Transform into someone else

Villain Card

Hidden Identity: Jimmy Powerboots (previously known as Jimmy- Boy Wonder)
Birth Name: Timothy Jonathan Sykes (nicknamed Jimmy)
Age: 9
Height: 4 feet, 1 inch
Weight: 65 pounds
Sidekick: unknown
Known Allies: Peter Powerhats
Source of Power: Boots

Powers

Boot Color	Boot Picture	Power
Black	Cracked ground	Powerstomp
Purple	One leg on each side of a wall	Walk through walls
Orange	Floating bananas	Move objects with mind
Red	Boots with flame	Rocket boots
White	5 identical stick figures	Clone himself
Yellow	Half-boy here, half-boy there	Teleport
Blue	Wall of water	Control water
Brown	Big ear	Super senses
Green	Computer	Computer hacking
Red/blue/yellow	Wires	Skills with electronics
Gray	Yellow pages	Find anyone in the world
Gold & black checkered	Clock	Speed up time

Acknowledgements

With Nikki Powergloves the first person I have to thank is my mom, Nancy Estes. She was so supportive of this book and the whole Nikki Powergloves series and put up with me writing a book every few weeks and immediately sending each to her to read. She always encouraged me to keep working on this series as she saw the potential it had to put a smile on a whole bunch of kids' faces—I truly hope it does.

As always, thank you to my wife, Adele, for being there for me when I don't see the light at the end of the tunnel or when I am frustrated with formatting my books when we're trying to watch a movie.

A huge thanks to my marketing team at shareAread, particularly Nicole Passante and Karla Calzada, who seem to believe in me even when I don't. You also deserve a special thanks for tackling the children's market with me, which I think we are all learning is a whole difference ballgame than young adult.

Thanks to my incredible team of kid beta readers and their moms, who gave me so much positive feedback to keep me excited about the project, while adding in awesome constructive feedback so I could make *Nikki Powergloves* even better. So thank you to D'vora Gelfond and her niece Maia Farina, Adriana Noriega and her son Jordan, Brooke Del Vecchio and her son Anthony, Laurie Love and her daughter Ericka, and Gabriela Racine and her son Carlos.

Thank you to my cover artists/designers at Winkipop Designs, you seem to be able to handle everything I throw at you so perfectly! I'm truly lucky to have you on my team and as friends.

And most importantly I'd like to thank all the kids out there who love to read, you are awesome!! Keep on reading and using your imaginations and loving life the way you do!

Discover other books by David Estes available through the author's official website:

http://davidestes100.blogspot.com or through select online retailers including Amazon.

<u>Children's Books by David Estes</u>

The Nikki Powergloves Adventures:
Nikki Powergloves- A Hero is Born
Nikki Powergloves and the Power Council
Nikki Powergloves and the Power Trappers
Nikki Powergloves and the Great Adventure
Nikki Powergloves vs. the Power Outlaws (coming in 2013!)

<u>Young-Adult Books by David Estes</u>

The Dwellers Saga:
Book One—The Moon Dwellers
Book Two—The Star Dwellers (Coming September 30 2012!)

The Evolution Trilogy:
Book One—Angel Evolution
Book Two—Demon Evolution
Book Three—Archangel Evolution

Connect with David Estes Online

Facebook:

http://www.facebook.com/pages/David-Estes/130852990343920

Author's blog:

http://davidestesbooks.blogspot.com

Smashwords:

http://www.smashwords.com/profile/view/davidestes100

Goodreads author page: http://www.goodreads.com/davidestesbooks

Twitter:

https://twitter.com/#!/davidestesbooks

About the Author

After growing up in Pittsburgh, Pennsylvania, David Estes moved to Sydney, Australia, where he met his wife, Adele. Now they travel the world writing and reading and taking photographs.

A SNEAK PEEK
NIKKI POWERGLOVES and the Power Council
Available now anywhere e-books are sold or in print on Amazon.com!

1

Mr. Miyagi barks away the storm

"Checkmate! Whoop whoop!" Spencer yelled gleefully.

"You win again," Mrs. Nickerson said.

Nikki was watching TV while her best friend, Spencer, played chess with her mom. She was bored, but not because her friend was talking more to her mom than to her. She was bored because it had been two days since she had done anything amazing.

"I gotta get outta here," Nikki mumbled. A cartoon flashed across the screen, and although she was looking at the TV, she wasn't really seeing it. She was too busy thinking.

"What did you say, honey?" her mom asked.

Nikki turned her head. Her mom was looking at her strangely. She forgot that she had spoken. "Oh, nothing, Mom. I'm just bored, that's all."

Her mother grinned sheepishly. "I'm sorry, dear. I guess I've been stealing Spencer away all afternoon."

"It's okay. It's not that. I think I just need to get out of the house," Nikki said.

Mrs. Nickerson laughed. "The rain doesn't seem like it will stop anytime soon, Nikks. You might just have to find a way to amuse yourself indoors."

Nikki groaned. *Ugh*. Rain, rain, and more rain. All day, all night. For two days straight it had poured down rain in Cragglyville. Nikki could have stopped it, could have made the sun come out again, but she and Spencer agreed that she shouldn't. The news reporters were saying how good the rain was for the farmers, how they really needed it. And Nikki didn't want to cause the farmers any trouble. Especially because one of the farmers was a close friend of hers, Farmer Miller.

But still, she was tempted to do something about it. Now that she was a superhero, Nikki wasn't used to having to wait so long for adventure. *Two days of rain is a long time*, she thought. Surely it was enough for the farmers. Right?

As she considered stopping the rain, Nikki stared at her wrist. Tight against her skin was a thin, metal bracelet holding a single round, blue gem. *Her powerbracelet*. Any moment it could flash, calling her into action—Nikki Powergloves to the rescue! Instead, it just stared right back at her, as if it was saying, "Sorry, Nikki. Nobody needs your help today."

Spencer plopped down next to her on the couch. She glanced up at him, but not before he saw that she was staring at her bracelet.

Nikki said, "So…my mom beat you at chess one out of five today, huh?"

Spencer leaned toward her and whispered, "I let her win, but don't tell her." His eyes gleamed mischievously.

"I thought so," Nikki said, smiling for the first time in hours. *What would I do without Spencer?* she asked herself. He had been her best friend for as long as she could remember. He had also been a genius for as long as she could remember. She was lucky to have him, especially now that she was a superhero. In her first week as a hero, she had battled against her arch nemesis, a boy villain who called himself Jimmy Powerboots. She might never have defeated him if not for Spencer's help. He was a good friend.

Motioning to Nikki's bracelet, Spencer said, "You hoping for an adventure today, Grasshopper?"

"Anything to get out of the house," Nikki said. "Are you sure it won't be sunny anytime soon?"

Spencer began humming to himself, his usual signal that he was thinking. After ten seconds, he said, "Well, the weather is very unpredictable, but I was looking at the radar earlier today, and it is showing rain for at least another couple of days."

Nikki groaned again. "I don't know if I'll last that long!"

Overhearing their conversation, Nikki's mom said, "Don't be so dramatic, Nikki. Why don't you kids just play a game while I start getting dinner ready?"

"Good idea!" Nikki said, grabbing Spencer's hand and pulling him off the couch, across the room, and up the stairs. Over her shoulder, she yelled, "Thanks, Mom! We'll play Monopoly or something in my room."

As soon as they were in her room, Nikki shut the door. A ball of fur stirred on the carpet in front of her. A low whine issued from the furry creature. "Sorry, Mr. Miyagi, I didn't mean to wake you," Nikki said. Nikki's dog licked his chops and then yawned as his eyes slowly opened. The gray Scottish terrier smiled sleepily when he saw Spencer, who promptly scratched him behind the ears.

"That's a good boy," Spencer said in a high-pitched voice. "Where are your games, Nikki?"

"For being a genius, you're kind of slow sometimes, Spence," Nikki said.

Spencer cocked his head to the side, confused, like he was trying to make sense of what Nikki had said. "You mean we didn't come up here to play Monopoly?" he said. He sounded disappointed.

"Nope. We're gonna fix this little weather problem."

"Are you sure that's such a good idea?"

Nikki paused to think about it. Then she said, "Yes! It's a great idea! In fact, it's my duty because if I don't stop it soon this whole town might flood. I am just trying to help."

Spencer said, "Okay. If you say so, Bumble-Muppet."

Nikki laughed. Even though she was used to the way Spencer always called her funny names and yelled crazy things, he still managed to surprise her every now and then with a really silly one. "Bumble-Muppet?" she said.

Spencer shrugged. "It's a gift, what can I say?"

Nikki giggled. "Now, back to this little weather problem…"

She reached in her pocket and extracted a small box. Both Mr. Miyagi and Spencer watched her curiously. She placed the box on the carpet in the middle of her room, well away from the walls or furniture. Then she stood back and used a string attached to the lid to open the box. The tiny box, which was really a miniature chest, suddenly exploded outwards, ballooning in size until it was more than half as tall as Nikki.

Nikki was given the treasure chest earlier that summer. The giver was a strange talking creature that called itself a Weeble, but looked more like a cross between a beaver and a porcupine. When Nikki met the Weeble her life had changed forever, because inside the box was a more incredible prize than she could have possibly imagined.

With Spencer and her dog still watching her, Nikki reached inside the chest and removed two gloves. They looked rubbery and were colored black and yellow. A picture of a lightning bolt was etched on the palms. Nikki tugged the gloves onto each hand. As always, they fit perfectly.

Just in case her mom came into her room, Nikki pushed the heavy lid back onto the chest. As soon as it snapped into place, the magical chest began to bubble and then shrink, getting smaller and smaller until it was no taller than a quarter. Nikki pocketed the tiny box for safekeeping.

Scooting onto her bed, she crawled across to the window. Spencer followed and settled in on his knees, shoulder to shoulder with her. Mr. Miyagi leapt onto the bed and pushed his head between their hips, so he could see out into the yard. Lasers of rain fell from the sky, coating the plants, lawn furniture, and grass in wetness. The sky was dark, full of smoggy clouds that seemed intent on covering the blue skies forever or maybe even longer. Although it was the late afternoon, it felt like the dead of night.

Nikki concentrated. In her mind swirled images of the clouds moving away. She could picture a beam of sunlight bursting through the storm, providing a small measure of warmth and light. Then she pictured another sunbeam, and another, and another, until the sky was full of light, the sun shining brightly on the little town of Cragglyville.

Mr. Miyagi barked. Nikki looked at the sky. A final burst of rain poured from the heavens and then the storm began to slow. The clouds parted, moving impossibly in all directions. Mr. Miyagi kept barking at the sky, as if he wanted to chase the clouds away with his voice. The fat droplets of rain went on a diet and were soon thin and misty. Just before the rain stopped completely, a glorious burst of color arced across the sky! A perfect rainbow, full of reds and blues and yellows, streamed overhead.

"Wow!" Spencer said. "Jumpin' banana skins, that's incredible!"

Mr. Miyagi barked once more, as if to say, "I love rainbows!"

There was a knock at the door and then it opened. Nikki turned to see her mom enter the room. "What's all the fuss?" she asked. "I heard Mr. Miyagi barking."

Nikki smiled and said, "It was nothing, Mom. Mr. Miyagi was just barking away the storm." Mr. Miyagi wagged his tail and grinned proudly.

2

Spencer wears his underwear on his head

There was still a full hour before dinner would be ready and Nikki planned to take full advantage of it. As she and Spencer stepped outside, Nikki sighed when she felt the warmth of the sunshine on her face. A light breeze wafted in from the north, gently cooling everything in its path. The weather was perfect, but Nikki was not surprised. After all, she had made it that way.

Nikki said, "Want to go for a ride?"

Spencer's face lit up. "Do you really mean it? Yippee!"

"Is your mom home?" Nikki asked.

Spencer said, "No, she's working a double shift."

"Good. Let's go to your place so we can put on our disguises."

The pair walked down the block and entered Spencer's house through the side door, for which he had a key. The door led into a small, dark basement, which was littered with cardboard boxes and smelled like dust and cleaning products. Spencer reached up and pulled a string, turning on a lonely light bulb.

"Okay, let's hurry," Nikki said. "We don't have much time."

Nikki quickly opened the magical powerchest and pulled out a light blue glove. It had a picture of a bird on it. She was still wearing one of her black and yellow gloves to make sure the sun would keep shining. Next she dug out two pairs of shoes and some clothing. She handed Spencer his black sweatpants and a black t-shirt that said "Certified Genius" on it. A few days earlier, Spencer had insisted on having a disguise, too.

"What about my glasses?" he said.

"Oh, sorry," Nikki replied. Reaching back into the chest, she extracted a pair of dark sunglasses.

Spencer put them on first. "Thanks. Now close your eyes, Nikki."

"You first," she said.

Spencer clamped his eyes tightly shut beneath the sunglasses.

"No peeking," Nikki said sharply.

With practiced precision, she changed out of her shorts and t-shirt into the clothing she got from the powerchest. The new blue shorts were rimmed by a white stripe, which matched her blue and white tennis shoes. Her shirt was yellow, with a light blue picture of a glove on it, beneath her superhero initials, NP. Covering the rest of the shirt were various colored symbols, each of which represented another one of her many powers. The t-shirt design had been Spencer's idea. Lastly, she tied her brown ponytail around the front of her head, covering her eyes. She clipped the end of the ponytail behind her ear to hold it in place.

"Okay, you can open your eyes, Spence. Can you help me with my eye holes?"

She felt Spencer's hand touch her face and then she could see again, through holes that Spencer had burrowed in her ponytail. In each hole he inserted a small plastic circle. Nikki felt like she was looking through funny goggles, but she didn't mind. Sometimes superheroes had to make sacrifices to keep their identities a secret.

"Now your turn," Nikki said, closing her eyes.

She heard scuffling and shuffling, and then a minute later Spencer said, "Presto chango!" It's what he always said when he was finished putting on his costume.

Nikki opened her eyes and saw Spencer grinning at her, his mouth wide and full of teeth. His braces gleamed under the bright exposed light bulb. She grinned back at him. He looked funny wearing all black, especially because of the sunglasses. It was like he was a secret spy or something.

"Ready?" Nikki said, as she pushed her hand into the blue glove.

"I was born ready!" Spencer said.

They marched up the basement stairs and into the empty kitchen. As they passed through the tiled dining area, Nikki couldn't help but to remember how Jimmy Powerboots had looked the last time she had seen him. At the time, Nikki had thought she might have killed him when she used her powers to hit him in the head with a lightning bolt. His face had been as pale as a ghost. Nikki had cried, because she didn't want to hurt anyone, not even a villain. Eventually, however, Jimmy had woken up and Nikki had flown him far away, but only after taking his powerboots from him. Without them, he wouldn't be able to cause any more trouble.

Then, just a few days ago, he had called her with some news. Jimmy had a new friend named Peter Powerhats, and one of his powers was the ability to find lost powerchests. When Nikki and Spencer were out playing, Jimmy and Peter had snuck behind Nikki's house and retrieved Jimmy's powerboots from where Nikki had hidden them in the backyard.

Nikki shivered as she opened the back door, even though the air outside was warm and humid. She knew Jimmy would be coming back to Cragglyville to get his revenge, and he would probably bring his friend Peter with him. Nikki tried not to think about it. Right now, she just wanted to fly!

Nikki kneeled in the grass in Spencer's fenced-in backyard. "Hop on," she said.

Luckily, Spencer was smaller than Nikki, and she could easily give him a piggyback ride. For some reason, it was even easier when she was flying. On her back, he felt as light as a feather. Once she felt Spencer's legs around her waist and his arms around her neck, she yelled, "Lift off!" and sprang into the air.

Magically, gravity could not hold her, and instead of crashing back to the ground, her body continued upwards, as she rocketed through the air with Spencer hanging on tightly. "Wheeeee!" he screamed. Soon they were high above the earth, twisting and turning and flipping and spinning. After a few minutes of playing on the breeze, Nikki settled into a gentle cruise across the town. Far below them, Nikki spotted a little boy eating an ice cream cone. He saw them too and waved. Nikki waved back, but Spencer kept his hands tightly around her so he wouldn't fall off.

Nikki loved flying and she was good at it. She could dive close to the ground and then rise back up rapidly. She could dart and cut and duck and dive around trees and houses and anything else that got in her way. She could land as softly as a butterfly and take off as powerfully as a rocket ship. She could spin and twirl and flip in the air like an Olympic gymnast. Nikki felt like she was born to fly.

Nikki cruised over some of the surrounding farmland and then turned and headed back toward town. As she was about to enter Cragglyville, her powerbracelet began to glow, turning from silver to bright white. Someone needed her help!

She flew over Cragglyville, scanning the streets.

The little boy who had been eating the ice cream was still there, but he was surrounded by two other boys. One of them had stolen his half-eaten ice cream cone and smashed it on the sidewalk. The other one was holding his arms and laughing. From high in the air, Nikki couldn't see who they were.

"Bullies!" Spencer yelped. "We've got to help him!"

Nikki nodded and started to dive for the ground, but then stopped when she saw one of the local shop owners emerge from his store and start yelling at the two bullies. The man was tall and strong. Hovering in the air, Nikki watched to see whether the bullies would leave the boy alone now that an adult had gotten involved.

To her surprise, one of the boy's suddenly began to grow bigger, until he was as tall and strong as the shop owner. If that wasn't amazing enough, the boy then grew even bigger, becoming a giant in mere seconds. He towered over the shop owner, making him look like a midget in comparison. It was then that Nikki noticed he was wearing a mask.

Nikki swooped in to get a closer look and her breath caught in her throat when she saw who the other boy was. Wearing a black cape, black mask, and mismatched boots—one blue and one yellow—there was no mistaking the identity of the boy: *Jimmy Powerboots was back in Cragglyville*. And he had brought company. The hulking boy beside him had to be Peter Powerhats. The giant was wearing a neon-green baseball cap, which, based on his name, had to be the source of his power.

Before Nikki could get any closer, Peter the Giant had grabbed the shop owner with one big hand and was shaking him. The little boy had wisely run away and was cowering behind a nearby mailbox.

Peter carried the man over to a yellow fire hydrant on the sidewalk, setting him down onto it. Next, Jimmy pointed a finger at the hydrant. Nikki could see him laughing as he did it. The hydrant burst open, sending a mountain of water high into the air. The shop owner went flying, carried upwards by the power of the water. Luckily, he was able to grab a tree branch as he flew past, clutching the bark like a lifeline. He hung on for dear life, his feet dangling helplessly in the empty air.

Nikki knew she had to do something fast or he would fall and break his legs.

Staying out of Jimmy's field of vision, Nikki flew over a building and into an alley, where she lowered Spencer onto his feet. "Stay here," she said.

"No, I need to help you, I'm your sidekick," Spencer said seriously.

"Spence, I don't have time for this. It's too dangerous for you." Without another word, she jumped in the air and raced off. She whipped over the building and shot toward the tree, where the poor man was still hanging on for dear life.

As she passed by the leafy branches she grabbed the big man by the waist and pulled him free. Seconds later he was back on the ground, safe and sound but very scared. "Thank you, Nikki, thank you," he said, while trying to catch his breath.

"No time to talk," Nikki said. She turned around to see Jimmy and Peter staring at her, laughing.

"I knew you'd come," Jimmy said. "You could never stay away from someone in trouble." He started to walk toward her. Peter followed after him, his giant legs looking more like tree trunks than the stubby legs of a nine-year-old boy.

Nikki knew she was in trouble. She was outnumbered two to one, and she only had her flying glove and her weather glove. With Jimmy and Peter moving toward her, she didn't have time to open her powerchest to access any of her other powers. She didn't think being able to fly and control the weather would be enough to stop them. Her mind was racing as she tried to think what to do. "Think, think, think," she said to herself. *If only Spencer was here*, she thought. He would know what to do.

That's when she heard a crazy sound. "Boogey-woogey-woogey-woogey!" a voice yelled from around the corner. And then he was there, a black streak running toward Jimmy and Peter. It was Spencer. But his disguise looked different. There was something on his head. Something white. Something cotton.

Underwear.

Spencer was wearing white underwear on his head. Not boxers or briefs, but tighty-whities. His face looked crazy, his eyes bugged out and his mouth twisted like he was completely out of his mind. His tongue wagged from his lips like an old hound dog.

"Argabargargabargargabarga!" he roared.

Jimmy and Peter turned away from Nikki, their eyes wide with terror as the strange pipsqueak of a boy charged them, displaying his private clothing like a crown atop his head.

Nikki's first instinct was to fly to Spencer and grab him before he got himself hurt. But then she realized what he was doing. He was distracting them. He had given her one chance to defeat them, and she couldn't waste it.

While Jimmy and Peter were looking the other way, Nikki reached in her pocket and retrieved her powerchest. Moments later it was open and she was sifting through the rubbery powergloves, trying to decide which ones to use. Quickly making a decision, she ripped off her light blue and black/yellow gloves and threw them in the chest. Then she snatched two other gloves, one gray and one white. The white glove had a snowflake on it and the other had no picture at all. She put them on.

The moment the gray glove covered her hand, she disappeared. She wasn't gone from Cragglyville, but she had become invisible.

A raindrop splashed onto her face. Nikki craned her head to look at the sky, which had darkened, as pregnant black rainclouds moved overhead. The sun, which was only able to shine on Cragglyville while Nikki was wearing her weather glove, was now hidden behind towers of stormy pillows. Another raindrop beat on Nikki's cheek. And then another. And another. One dripped into her eye, temporarily blurring her vision. She was about to get very wet. But that didn't matter—she needed to save Spencer.

Nikki surveyed the scene in front of her. Spencer had reached Peter Powerhats first and was swinging his small fists at him, trying to punch

166

him in the knees, but Peter had extended one of his long arms and was holding Spencer's head, keeping him far enough away that he couldn't reach him. Jimmy was laughing and kept spraying Spencer with water from the fire hydrant, using only his finger to direct the water at her genius sidekick.

Nikki sprang into action just as the heavens exploded, cascading torrents of rain onto the streets. In seconds she was drenched, her invisible clothes sticking to her invisible skin as the rain lashed at her invisible arms and hands. But Nikki didn't let it stop her. She raced toward where Spencer was being abused by Peter, splashing through puddles and soaking her socks and shoes. When she was ten steps away she aimed her white glove at him. A beam of whiteness spouted from her glove, coating the giant villain from head to toe in a block of ice.

Spencer gawked at the ice sculpture in front of him. "Great work, Nikks!" he yelled, whirling around to find her. Of course, he couldn't see her. Because no one could see her. Because she was invisible.

Jimmy, who was dripping with water, ran over to Peter's frozen body, and reached out to touch him. Nikki took aim with her finger again—she was going to freeze Jimmy, too. But right when the white laser shot from her glove, Jimmy and Peter disappeared. They were gone, like magic. It was as if they had never been there. The ice beam collided harmlessly with a mailbox, instantly turning it to ice. Nikki and Spencer were left alone in the street, as fat raindrops pelted them from above.

"Wowsers!" Spencer yelled. "If monkeys had wings it wouldn't be cooler than what you just did! Where are you anyway?"

Remembering she was still invisible, Nikki pried off her gray glove. She appeared. "I'm here, Spence."

Spencer walked to her, hopping over small puddles that got in his way. When he reached her, he put a wet arm around her and said, "Good job, Nikki. You did great."

Nikki smiled. "Thanks, Spence. But I couldn't have done it without you. That was some entrance!" She giggled when she looked at his head. A pair of sopping wet white underwear clung to his hair like a swim cap. "Where on earth did you get the underwear? You couldn't possibly have had time to take them off and then put all your clothes back on."

Spencer flashed a toothy smile. "I had them in my pocket, just in case. You never know when you are going to need a fresh pair!"

Nikki laughed and hugged her friend. "So much for our sunny day. Let's get home and dry off."

2/17 7LR

41937414R00094

Made in the USA
Lexington, KY
02 June 2015